the consequence of rejection

#1 NEW YORK TIMES BESTSELLING AUTHOR

RACHEL VAN DYKEN

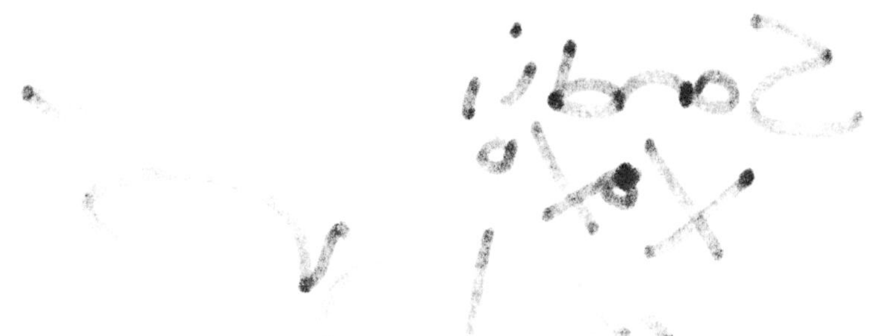

The Consequence of Rejection
The Consequences Series
Book 4
by Rachel Van Dyken

THE CONSEQUENCE OF REJECTION

ISBN-13: 978-1-7321428-1-7
Cover Art by Jena Brignola
Formatting by Jill Sava, Love Affair With Fiction

dedication

To all the readers who wanted this story and encouraged me to dive into the crazy head of Max one last time…I love you guys!

prologue

Jason

I TIPPED BACK the lukewarm Corona and glanced at the flickering TV. Alone. Again.

A knock sounded at the door.

I ignored it and reached for another slice of pizza. How long had I been sitting in my living room? I hadn't a clue.

I'd lost track of a lot of things in the past week.

My truck door, for one — my fault.

My heart — her fault.

My balls — the universe's fault and an unfortunate run-in with lightning… more to come on that later.

And finally — my ability to move on.

It's easy the first time you move on from a lost love. Life happens, days go by, and you chalk it up to the fact that you were immature and stupid. Hell, you were eighteen. What did you even know at eighteen? I'd been a virgin until her.

So honestly? Nothing. I hadn't known a damn. Thing.

The second time you miss that opportunity to love — well, that's when things go to shit.

Exhibit A: my parents' house. Takeout boxes littered every inch of space, beer bottles totem-poled the boxes, and something smelled.

I sniffed my armpit.

That something was me.

I glanced down the hallway. *Too much effort in trying to get clean. What the hell was the point anyway?* She was gone. Again. I was alone. Again.

And you know the really sick part?

Before she'd come stomping back into my life, I'd been completely okay with it! I'd finally settled into my job at the local police department. I had great friends, was remodeling up my parents' house, and I had the promise of a goat—

Don't ask.

The point? Everything had been fine until Maddy Summers decided to screw me over.

The knocking got louder.

"Not home!" I yelled.

The door burst open.

Not my best friend, Max, walked into the house, his feet kicking empty boxes. My best friend Colton, followed along with Reid, Max's brother, goat tucked under his arm and his nose scrunched up as if I was the animal, not the crazy mammal he was carrying.

"Dude." Max shook his head. "You stink."

Colton winced as a piece of pizza, that had somehow found its way to my ceiling, fell to the ground, narrowly missing his shoes. "Jason…"

"Guys!" I forced a smile. "I'm fine!"

"You're not fine!" Max yelled. "You're a pig in your own

filth! You smell, your house is a mess, and I saw at least two good-sized rats leaving through the front door — meaning you've even managed to scare rodents! Pull yourself together!"

I burped. "You gonna slap me now?"

"Do it." Colton crossed his arms. "Or at least hose him off."

"Please!" I shouted. "This from three happily married guys? Let me rot in my filth!"

"He's drunk," Max announced. "He didn't even chase her!"

"What's the point?" I felt the familiar sting of rejection hit me square in the chest. "Things are better this way." I didn't tell them that her car was gone; that when I'd called her work the day after being arrested by my partner at the precinct, she'd taken a week off. And when I'd stopped by her parents', they'd just given me a pathetic look as if they hadn't known what to say.

I should have gotten her number.

I should have run like hell.

"So, go after her." This from Colton.

"And say what? Choose me? Stay with me? She's left me twice, guys. She's not coming back."

Max sighed and kicked a box in my direction, then reached out and patted my hand. Aw, he was comforting me. That was nice of him to—

"What the hell!" I screamed, as Max slapped me across the face twice, then pulled his fist back as if he was going to beat the shit out of me.

"Get off your ass, or so help me God, I'm calling your grandmother!"

"No!" I shot to my feet. "You wouldn't."

Colton shivered. "He would."

"Jason?" an elderly voice chimed in from the door. "Grandma's moving in!"

My eyes widened.

"Those are your choices," Max said, looking pleased. "Either you chase your woman, or Grandma moves in. We already packed her shit."

"What?" Grandma yelled. "What was that, Maxy?"

"You look so fit!" He beamed.

She did a little twirl, then put on her bright red lipstick. "I've been dancing."

"Oh, it shows." Max winked.

I groaned.

"So, shall we help you shower, or are you and Grandma new roomies?" Colton asked.

I glared at both of them. "Shower. Now."

"That's the spirit!" Max clapped. "Let's go get your woman!"

chapter one

"When life gives you lemons — make beer! What? You thought I was going to say lemonade? Idiots. When one is down in the dumps and thinking of jumping off a bridge, the very last thing that would help would be lemonade. Beer, on the other hand? When has anyone ever regretted making beer? Or drinking it, for that matter? That's what I thought."

~From Max Emory's Guide to Dating and Other Important Life Lessons

Jason

Four weeks earlier

"That's the fifth call this week," I grumbled aloud, as I slowly got out of the SUV and shook my head at the scene in front of me. Political signs had been randomly showing up on people's yards. Normally, it wouldn't be a big deal since it was campaign season.

But these signs were of Max Emory and his megawatt smile, with two thumbs way up. And the tagline? *I'm not running for anything. I just wanted a sign too!*

With our damn luck, he was somehow going to get voted into office, and that would be the beginning of the end. One day, mayor of the city, the next day President of the United States. My body gave an involuntary shudder — God forbid. I needed a damn piece of wood to knock on. Hell, make that a salt-shaker and a freaking box of Lucky Charms.

Grunting, I pulled the stupid sign out of the yard and tossed it into the back seat of the still-running SUV.

My phone rang.

It was as if he knew.

He being Max.

What did he do? Put tracking devices in the signs? I was almost afraid to ask, because the explanation would most likely be extensive, and I had a dinner date.

Correction, I had a hot dinner date.

With Blanche.

One of my grandmother's best friends — the one who still miraculously had all her teeth and only one hearing aid, bless her heart. I called her hot because she used to give me Hot Tamales candy when I was a kid, and when my mouth burned and went tingly all at once, she said that meant I was on a hot date.

Don't ask me how long I associated candy with hot girls. Let's just say the damn woman classically conditioned me to salivate whenever a chick walked by. It took me years to get over that embarrassing condition that my best friend Colton often told kids in our class was an allergic reaction to my own spit.

Asshole.

"Yeah?" I barked into the phone.

"You're moving my signs again," Max said in a bored voice. He was the CEO of the Emory hotel empire and clearly had way too much time on his hands. Recently married, you'd think he'd be too busy to eat lunch, let alone put up signs ninety minutes from his penthouse apartment in Manhattan.

"Max…" I prayed for patience. "…I'm an officer of the law. I deal with thugs, drugs, prostitutes, and murder."

"You forgot speeding tickets."

"Max… " I warned.

"Speeding is an offense too. So is stealing. What about the kleptomaniacs? They don't even get an honorable mention?"

"Why?" I pinched the bridge of my nose. "Why put up the signs? You do realize it's a waste of my time and your money."

He burst out laughing; it sounded more like an evil cackle. "That's funny — you're funny. You know that? Waste of money." He continued to laugh. "And time? When was the last time you had an arrest, Jason?"

I clenched my teeth. "We had a streaker after the Yale game last night."

"You get shot?"

"No."

He sighed. "That's too bad."

"That I'm alive?"

A loud yawn echoed across the phone. "Anyway, enough of your life. It makes me too depressed. Did you get all the signs yet?"

I glanced at the yards around me. "There are more?"

"According to my GPS, yes."

"You're wasting taxpayers' money!"

He was silent and then said very slowly, "Jason, you need to get the final sign. The future of our very world depends on it!"

I climbed into my SUV and slammed the door. Sarcastic nightmare. "Goodbye, Max."

"Yes!" he yelled. "Now you've got it. We'll be saying sayonara to the planet Earth if you don't go get that last sign." He was exaggerating, being a pain in the ass, and costing taxpayers money. The guy literally just wanted to make a sign with his name on it. Apparently owning the biggest hotel empire in the world wasn't enough — well that, and he said he was going to make my life Hell until I settled down and found happiness, as if I wasn't already happy! I clutched my phone tightly, nearly breaking it in half. I was DAMN happy. Damn it!

"Where is it?"

"How should I know? Do you really think I actually drive down there and put those little suckers in the ground?

I could get a sliver, and those little shits hurt."

"The horror."

"No..." he sighed, completely ignoring me, "...I pay my new assistant to do that shit."

Never thought I'd feel so sorry for an individual I'd never met.

"Okay fine, I'll tell you."

"Wait, I thought you didn't know."

"I lied."

"Max!" A headache was coming on already; a Max-induced headache that I, and my circle of friends, had nicknamed a Maxache. Nothing worked on it, not even the strongest of drugs.

Alcohol took the edge off.

But being drunk at work was frowned upon.

"It's a small red house just off Main and First. You can't miss it. There's a flag in the front yard, waving proud the red, white, and blue. I swear it just evokes feelings of patriotism."

"The red house?" My stomach clenched. "With the flagpole and white porch?

"Hey!" Max said, a little too cheerfully. "You know it, then?"

"Max." *Yup, definitely a Maxache.* "What the hell did you do?"

"Do?"

"*She* lives there."

"She?"

"I refuse to say her name out loud."

"Ah, it's one of those Bloody Mary things, got it. All right then, have fun and take some pictures of the sign. I'm working on my Twitter campaign this afternoon."

"Go to Hell, Max!"

I hung up.

And stared at the steering wheel.

The bastard was sneaky, I'd give him that. He always came off as slightly stupid and way too arrogant for his own good. But he was brilliant.

That, my friends, was the problem.

Nothing good came from a multimillion-dollar genius with unlimited resources and time on his hands… A genius who just so happened to think playing with his friends' lives was an actual hobby.

It all started at my wedding last year.

A wedding, I'll admit, Max saved me from.

A marriage from Hell would be a generous understatement.

He'd shown up, pretended to be my sister's fiancé, helped Colton my best friend, finally see the light about my sister, Milo, and ended up almost drowning me in the pool.

By the end of the weekend, I had two black eyes, a limp, and on Sunday, woke up drunk in a water fountain, with a frog sitting on my chest and a hangover that pounded my skull for two straight days.

I still think he drugged me.

He still claims all whiskey tastes that funny.

Regardless, somehow that solidified his spot in our family. He went on a dating show, compliments of my own personal revenge for nearly killing me, and I'd been biding my time until it all came back to haunt me.

Never in my wildest imagination did I think he would stoop this low, though.

Never.

With sweaty palms, I put the SUV in reverse, turned around in the subdivision, then slowly crept along, prolonging the inevitable… when I would have to see *Ethel.*

chapter two

"If something is easy, that means you didn't earn it. Wow, just went deep on you, didn't I? Example: When getting the girl is easy — when the girl says yes right away — wave your hand in front of her face. She may be blind, home skillet. If said girl furrows her eyebrows, check her pulse. Can't find her pulse? Aw, bless your heart, you've just hit on your first zombie. On a totally related note, the fate of the world is now in your hands. Badass, if you ask me."

~From Max Emory's Guide to Dating and Other Important Life Lessons

Jason

THE SMALL RED house came into view. I narrowed my eyes as a bead of sweat ran down my temple then slid into the collar of my shirt.

I pulled the safety off my Glock and slowly turned off the engine.

The sound of my feet hitting the gravel sounded like something out of a bad cop movie. Dirt swirled in slow motion around my ankles as I took my first step. My black shoes crunched on the remaining gravel as I made my way onto the small innocent-looking sidewalk.

Crows circled above the house, as if they KNEW.

A golden retriever waltzed down the street then, swear on Max's life, turned around with its tail between its legs.

The rocking chair on the front porch continued its back and forth motion as the screen door burst open.

I fingered my gun as perspiration my upper lip.

"Ethel." I said her name like the curse it was.

She sniffed the air then lowered her chin at me. "Jason." Her floppy grey hair waved in the wind as she peered over her thick, horn-rimmed glasses, her beady eyes seeing right through me.

My finger twitched.

"What are you doing out in these here parts?" Wrinkled bits of her red mumu hugged her calves; each time the wind picked it up, I caught sight of her pink fuzzy socks and weathered brown Birkenstocks.

"Oh, you know… just checking on my favorite town folk." I forced a smile, my eyes grazing the lawn until they landed on the last Max sign.

Bingo.

Sadly, it was at least twenty feet away.

Closer to Ethel than me.

It may as well have been in the depths of Hell.

I wondered, in that moment, if it would be better to just run, or, knowing Ethel, would she simply gallop after me, strike my head with a blunt object, and drag me into her house?

The sign mocked me as it caught sunlight and gleamed in my direction. The picture of Max appeared to be waving at me.

Sighing, I took a tentative step down the sidewalk. I wouldn't hear the end of it if Ethel happened to venture out this afternoon to get her mail, spot Max's face in her yard, only to turn around and scream about the city's inability to keep people off her property.

Let's just say, if her house was on fire, the fire department would ignore the call.

Illegal? Yes.

Horrific? Absolutely.

Necessary? You. Have. No. Idea.

Ethel ran this neighborhood. Children whispered about her around the campfires, and she'd already forced two police chiefs into retirement — before the age of fifty.

"Say, Ethel." I used a calm voice, one I saved for keeping people from jumping off buildings and going splat. I held out my hands. "I don't want any trouble. I just came to grab an illegal sign off your property."

"If you were doing your job, it wouldn't be on my property, now would it, Jason?"

I bit back a curse. *Damn it, Max!* "Now, Ethel, you know I can't sit out here in a lawn chair with a shotgun just waiting for trespassers."

"Last police chief did."

"He was fired."

She sniffed and looked away, crossing her arms. "Well, be quick about it, Jason. I'm plucking a bird out back."

I didn't ask.

I wasn't afraid of her answer. I was terrified she'd actually show me, and I'd never make it back to my SUV. They'd discover my battered body years later, a look of horror on my young face.

"Right." Slowly, I inched farther onto her property. Sweat continued to pour down my neck, soaking my shirt and making me curse the day police uniforms had been made of such thick cotton.

"Who's Max?" she asked, once my hands grazed the sign and pulled it up from its spot right in front of her porch.

I looked at the sign, slowly backed away, and answered, "He's you, only male and slightly younger."

"Sounds delightful!"

"You have no idea." I whistled low in my throat as I clutched the sign to my side and monitored her for any sudden movements. She may look slow, but the woman used to run track, so she knew how to run, and sadly, for those she chased, she rarely gave up.

"Made some tea." She sniffed, running her finger underneath her nose as if that was supposed to make me want tea and not throw up over the fact that she was currently examining something between her fingers and lifting it to her lips.

"Nope." I held back a gag. "I'm allergic."

"To tea?" she asked, still holding her treasure between her fingers. *Don't do it, woman. Don't do it!*

It happened in slow motion, the moment where her fingers came into contact with her mouth and that wicked tongue slipped out and… licked.

Damn those Cheerios I'd eaten this morning!

Gagging again, I looked away. I had to.

"You sure, Jason?"

"Positive." I barked out a cough, my stomach heaving almost as much as my balls at the seductive glance she was giving me. Backing up, my ass nearly collided with the SUV.

Ethel put her hands on her hips and tapped her foot. "No more signs, Jason, or I ain't voting for you come next election!"

"Not running for mayor yet," I said under my breath.

"What was that?"

"I think the lawn is wet!" I chuckled loudly. "All righty then, see ya, Ethel. A pleasure, as always."

"Bite me," she spat. She legitimately spat onto the front porch then turned around and barreled back into the hole she'd crawled out of.

My fingers slipped on the ignition, twice, before I finally turned the key, started the SUV, then peeled out from her driveway as if zombies were chasing me.

I drove in silence as my heartbeat slowly returned to normal, thank God. I was going to kill Max — then kill him again, just to make sure he was dead.

But first, I needed whiskey.

Thankfully, my shift was done, and I could easily make

my way over to the restaurant, sit at the bar, and down a few shots before my dinner date.

The woman may have to be my DD with as much shaking as I was doing in that damn SUV. How did Max even know of Ethel? It's not like I'd talked about my long-time nemesis around the dinner table.

Maybe it had been Milo or Colt who'd blabbed about how Ethel had hated me since I was born? She was the nurse who'd delivered me, and, shit you not, told my parents that I was going to be a tyrant because I'd peed on her.

I was three minutes old, lady. Give me a break! Babies pee!

Correction: Not Max. Max's first sentence was probably, *"And they shall name me Max, and I shall rule the world."*

"Aghhh!" I hit my steering wheel and then pulled into the parking lot of the restaurant.

chapter three

"Sometimes, I eavesdrop on conversations with my headphones on, you know, to not appear suspicious, and listen to life. It's quite amazing what loose-lipped soccer moms say when given seven shots of espresso and a baked good. My advice if you're shit out of luck in the love department and need a little pick me up? The coffee shop is a gold mine of information. Case in point, last year I learned how to stuff a turkey and found out how to get wine out of a tablecloth, all because Molly was having a bad day. Oh, and I got a free coffee for smiling at her. See? A smile: worth a thousand compliments. Sometimes in life, you just need to pause, listen to other conversations, invade, and make the world a better place, one yoga pants-wearing soccer mom at a time."

~From Max Emory's Guide to Dating and Other Important Life Lessons

Maddy

IT HAD BEEN a mistake, returning to New Haven. I'd known that the minute the thought crossed my mind. Heck, the minute I pulled into town it had taken every ounce of strength I had to pass the first few stoplights and navigate the familiar route to my parents' house.

The one right next to Jason Caro's.

The window I crawled into…

The window I crawled out of…

The roof I got drunk on for the first time…

The mailbox I hit while driving Jason's truck…

Memories had full-on assaulted me while I made my way around the little subdivision, but nothing was worse than seeing that driveway empty.

Because it was just another reminder that I'd left him; that I was the one who had freaked out, bailed, and run as fast as my legs could take me.

That driveway used to have his favorite red truck parked out front. He'd done all his own detail work on it and, to this day, I was pretty sure there was still a black mark on the cement where the exhaust had sputtered and stained.

"Ma'am?" A deep male voice barked in my direction. "I asked if the Caesar salad was gluten-free?"

I was at my new job.

As a waitress.

Daydreaming about my best friend/ex-boyfriend from high school, and waiting on people who paid more for a steak than I made in a year. I was officially back in the one place I couldn't leave fast enough. Well, that wasn't officially true. I'd left because I had no choice, but still, nobody liked admitting defeat.

"Um, actually no." I forced a polite smile and tucked my light strawberry blonde curls behind my ear. "It has croutons, so that's gluten."

I bit my tongue to keep from blurting out that all bread has gluten unless it said gluten-free. Maybe the diet was new to him.

The man's eyebrows drew together in a frown as he peered over his spectacles. "Can't you order gluten-free croutons?"

"We can…" I said helpfully, my feet aching from standing all day. I shouldn't have pulled a double shift, but I needed more money if I had any hope of moving out of my parents' house. "…but we don't have any available. I'm so sorry. Why don't you try the house salad? Or possibly the spinach with our house-made vinaigrette?"

"Well," he tossed the menu in my direction, "that just ruins my whole meal. I was hoping to enjoy a Caesar."

I ground my teeth together before answering, "How about I just have the chef make a Caesar without the croutons?"

"A Caesar…" the man repeated, low in his throat, "… without croutons?"

You'd have thought I'd just told him to celebrate the Fourth of July without a hotdog while I was running over the flag wearing an *I-heart-Canada* shirt.

"Oh, Pete." The woman sitting opposite of him waved her heavily jeweled hand and gripped her goblet. "You don't need the carbs."

"True." His mood changed dramatically as he lifted his wine into the air and clinked his glass against hers. "I'll take the salad without croutons and the New York sirloin, rare, with mashed potatoes and the asparagus, please."

She grinned her approval, her white teeth momentarily blinding me.

Blinking to regain my focus, I stared her down, waiting for her order.

"The same." She nodded then held up her hand. "Except, no dressing on the salad, no dairy in my potatoes, and make sure the meat is well-done."

That wasn't the same. At. All.

But again, I held my tongue. The last thing I needed was to get fired after a week on the job.

"Sure!" I nodded. "Got it."

"Aren't you going to write that down?" she chuckled, mockingly.

"Great idea." My lips were trembling from all the polite smiles I was trying to force. For some reason, her talking down to me made my gut clench and emotion clog my throat as I pulled out a pad of paper and scribbled down the order I'd already memorized.

It was demeaning.

It shouldn't be.

But it was.

And I deserved it. I'd run away and never looked back. My gut clenched again. So maybe I had looked back, but only because I'd had no choice. He'd left me no choice…

But to run.

Right?

I'd been so young. We'd both been.

I thanked them, walked off, and typed the order into the computer.

"Hey." Liza slipped by me carrying about ten empty beer bottles. They clanged together, nearly tipping over, before she set down her tray and put her hands on her hips. "You look horrible."

"Gee..." my shoulders slunk, "...thanks. That's just what every girl wants to hear on a Friday night, just before all the rich people barge in and start complaining over the fact that I didn't give them a choice between still or sparkling water."

Liza's blue eyes twinkled. "Cheer up. I just mean you don't look like your normal, peppy self."

"When have I ever been peppy?" I finished typing in the order and moved my head back and forth to stretch my neck out.

"You were peppy in high school," she pointed out while she dumped the beer bottles into the recycling bin and wiped off her tray.

I let out a pitiful groan. "I was a cheerleader in high school, who thought the world revolved around the next football game."

"Correction." Liza bent over and grabbed a pack of napkins then tossed them in my direction. I ripped the plastic wrapping open while she kept jabbering on. "You were a cheerleader in high school who thought the world revolved around Jason Caro."

My cheeks felt hot. "Shh... keep your voice down."

"What?" She glanced around the empty hallway leading into the kitchen. "You afraid he's going to hear you all the way on the other side of town? From the police station? And the main office? With his door shut?"

I held up my hand. "You've made your point."

Liza's easy grin didn't help the nerves suddenly attacking every inch of my body. I'd have to face him sooner or later. The town wasn't big enough for the both of us.

Damn it.

Liza gripped my shoulders with both hands. "Look at me."

I glanced down at my black ballet flats.

"Maddy."

Slowly, I lifted my chin, my gaze faltering as my lower lip trembled just slightly. Age had done a real number on my emotions. I could at least admit that much.

Sometimes, I still smelled his cologne. He'd always looked like he'd just stepped out of a GQ commercial, so it only made sense that the man had worn Burberry. Something that, even to this day, made my eyes mist over and my throat clog up with emotion which, in turn, always made the peppy perfume-counter women think I was having an allergic reaction to their spray.

Nope, just having trouble traveling down memory lane since I bulldozed it then ran over Jason, the equivalent of the perfect man, minus the whole accident-prone thing he'd always had going on. Though I'd always been under the impression it had been more his sister's bad timing and Jason's bad luck.

"It's okay to still think about him, you know. God only knows every other girl who's ever seen that perfectly sculpted face has entertained similar thoughts. Then again, maybe not *every* other girl, since you actually saw him naked."

Because that was helpful.

Visions of his abs clouded my vision until my chest hurt…

"What the hell are you doing?" He growled against my

mouth as I lifted his shirt higher and higher, until bronze-muscled skin greeted my cold fingers.

"I'm freezing." I nipped his lower lip. "Warm me up?"

"Always." He tugged his shirt from his body then removed mine.

"What are you doing?" I burst out laughing while he continued to strip down to his boxers then reached for my jean shorts.

His green eyes sparked with lust. "What? I thought you needed me to warm you up? I may have been kicked out of Cub Scouts, but I'm pretty sure I got this shit locked down. Skin to skin contact, the only way to save a life."

"And my life needs saving?"

"Desperately," he breathed, his hands making dizzy circles down my hips until I bucked against him, my body craving more of him — always more.

"But your parents—"

"Gone. Weekend getaway."

"Milo?"

"Dead."

"What?" I gasped.

"Chill," he laughed. "She's with Colt at some weird Star Wars convention-party-thing that I refused to dress up for."

"So..." My heart skipped in my chest. "...it's just you and me."

"And the dog." Jason nodded seriously. "But he swore to take all secrets to the grave."

I tilted my head in Ruff's direction. "Can we trust him?"

"He put his paw across the Bible and then winked when I gave him a bone. I think we're good."

Laughing, I tugged Jason closer.

"I love you, Maddy. I always will."

"I love you too," I whispered.

"Your face is really red right now," Liza pointed out.

"Sorry." I shook my head. "Just… thinking."

"About Jason?"

"Shh!" I waved my hands in front of me. "I doubt he even remembers me. It was a long time ago."

Liza arched her eyebrows and then jutted out her hip. "Whatever makes you feel better about leaving him high and dry that night."

"With one of his best friends," was the other part of the story she wasn't saying; maybe for my sake, possibly for hers, since it was actually her brother who'd been my ride out of town.

Who'd helped me lie.

And then insulted me straight after.

"Chin up." She slapped her rag against the countertop. Droplets of water hit her black pencil skirt. "And thanks for taking a double tonight. We would have been swamped without you."

"Of course," I murmured, as I forced my thoughts back to the present. Another waitress, Stella, ran around the corner, her eyes wide as saucers.

"Liza!" Stella's eyes watered as she glanced between the two of us. "She's here."

"She?" I asked.

"Damn." Liza scratched her head. Her sleek honeyed hair was pulled back into a tight, low ponytail. "Marcus is sick, and she always requests him for her table."

Stella nodded dumbly. Was she starting to cry? "What do we do?"

Whatever. I'd dealt with the worst of the worst customers;

nobody could be as bad as Mr. Gluten-Free-Crouton man. "I'll take the table."

Stella paled.

I let out a non-committal shrug. "Guys, how bad can it be?"

"She set Marcus on fire," Stella whispered.

"Twice," Liza added.

"Why?"

"Because she could." Stella shook her head slowly then repeated. "Because she could."

Liza rolled her eyes. "Stop being dramatic. Maybe she'll take a liking to Maddy? Either way, we have to serve her. It's the law."

"Great." Stella rubbed her hands down her black knit dress. "I'll be sure to remember that when I end up in prison because I strangled the old bat."

As if on cue, a busboy rounded the corner, his cheeks red, his hands shaking. "Does anyone have the right water for the witch? I'm pretty sure she thinks I just offered to poison her."

"Why would she think that?" I asked, getting seriously irritated with the snotty customer I'd have to serve.

"Because she said so…" He gulped. "…after she spat it back in my face."

"Oh, for the love." I swiped some pink lip gloss across my lips, glanced at my reflection via the window to make sure my wild hair was tamed, and straightened my back. "I'll take care of this. What table?"

"Six." The busboy made a cross motion in front of his chest then lowered his head. "As in six-six-six, you know?" He was either Catholic, or thinking of converting — all because of some insane, needy individual who had a God-complex.

Well, not tonight.

Because I was in a hell of a mood.

My feet hurt.

My heart ached.

And I couldn't stop thinking of the only love I'd ever had — and lost. I took long, purposeful steps toward the new table.

An elderly lady with gray hair was sitting regally with her chin lifted high, her jeweled hands holding up a white napkin as if inspecting it, and her red lipstick perfectly drawn across her pouty mouth. She looked to be around eighty, but I wasn't sure because of all the makeup she had on.

Her red dress wrapped tightly around a fit form, and her black shawl was snugly circling her neck, falling over her left shoulder.

"Good evening," I said in the bravest voice I could muster. "And welcome to Terra. I'm—"

The young gentleman with her turned around slowly.

"J-Jason?"

chapter four

"They call it 'a blast from the past' because most times, it feels like a literal electrical jolt to your heart. It's painful as hell, and somehow time even manages to slow itself down just so you can feel that much shittier for that much longer. My advice? You see a blast, you run past the past. Feel me?"

~From Max Emory's Guide to Dating and Other Important Life Lessons

Jason

"What are you doing here?" Regret mixed with heavy dread decided to pool around my midsection, making me feel as if I needed to either hurl, or punch something. Seeing her didn't just feel like shit — it was actual shit, as if someone had handed me a branding iron and told me to stick it in my mouth and bite down until my tongue fell off — that kind of shit.

"Um…" Maddy's cheeks stained pink as she glanced between Blanche and me.

"We need water," Blanche said in fast, clipped tones. "I prefer sparkling, but my date likes his still."

I stole a glance at Blanche. She'd never called me her date before, at least not out loud, and I knew by the immediate horrified reaction on Maddy's face that she'd assumed the worst.

That I was Blanche's date, in every sense of the word. When really, all I did was keep her company a few times a month when she was missing her husband because he was on a fishing trip, or when she needed to fill me in on town gossip. I'd been sitting here for mere minutes when she'd started drilling me about Max's signs getting posted everywhere.

My *date* reached across the table and gripped my hand in hers. "Isn't that right, pumpkin sauce?"

I fought back the growl building in my throat as I squeezed back my words from tumbling out of my mouth like gravel. "Right."

"Okay." Maddy swallowed, her strawberry hair bouncing along her smooth ivory skin. Her perfume was the same, coconut-toasted something that made my mouth water instantly. It's been said that scent is the strongest way to pull out a memory, but when it came to Maddy, it had always been her lips.

I compared lips to hers.

Mouths.

Shit. Who was I kidding? I compared every girl I'd ever kissed. And they always came up short. It was always stupid things too, like her upper lip was too large, her teeth too straight, too white. The closest I'd ever come to dating a girl seriously after my failed engagement had been Jenna.

But that had gone to hell in a handbasket the minute I found out she'd slept with Reid, Max's famous brother. No chance in Hell was I going to be sloppy seconds. Because, according to Max, once girls get with Reid, they either die unhappy and alone — or build creepy incense altars in his honor, in hopes to somehow win him back. *Um, no thanks.*

"Is there anything other than water that I can get you two?" Maddy's blue eyes met mine briefly before returning to the older woman.

Blanche being Blanche, , tilted her head to the side and said, "An alcoholic beverage would be nice, but the last young man who brought me whiskey didn't pour it correctly."

As if it takes a PhD to pour two fingers of whiskey.

"Hmm, well how about I bring the bartender over here and—"

"Did I ask for the bartender?" Blanche's penciled brows

shot up.

I leaned back and bit my tongue. She had never been prickly on date night, but it was possible she knew the whole backstory with me and Maddy. After I'd gotten drunk last year on New Year's, I'd begged Blanche for a *"matronly kiss,"* because apparently — and this is all coming from Max, who witnessed the entire charade — that was all I was good for. Pleasing the elderly.

Oh, and yeah… Blanche had gone ahead and done just that… kissed my mouth.

Max claimed it was the best damn kiss he'd ever seen.

Then again, Max has an actual bunker in his apartment for when the zombies attack so… grain of salt, you know?

Needless to say, Blanche hadn't been a fan.

"No, you didn't ask for the bartender." Maddy bit down on her lower lip.

I sucked in a breath and nearly choked on my tongue as I pounded my chest lightly and looked away, fighting to keep my expression void of emotion.

She'd left me.

Abandoned me.

And freaking accomplished it by getting into our mutual friend's Jeep with a wave goodbye and parting words

.

"One day you'll find someone who makes you happy. It just isn't me."

"And asshat makes you happy?" I pointed to Levi and shook my head, as his smug reflection in the mirror challenged me to fight.

"He does." Maddy nodded. "He makes me… feel things."

"Feel things?" I scoffed. "What the hell, Maddy? I think any guy with working parts can make you feel things."

"Other things," she added quickly. "Inside."

"You aren't making sense!"

"Look, he's really deep. We connect on a more..." she looked away, "...spiritual level."

"Bullshit! He thought church history was a class on fiction writing!"

"Hey!" Maddy shot me a defensive glare. "That wasn't his fault."

"Whatever." I held up my hands. "This is what you want?" I pointed at the brand-new Jeep. "Then go. But I don't want to ever see you again."

"Fine!"

"And Maddy?" I yelled as she stomped off.

"What?" Tears poured down her face, though she tried to wipe them away as fast as possible with her hands.

"You're dead to me."

My heart was dead. She'd stomped all over it, all over us, without so much as a backward glance. I could still smell the fuel as he hit the accelerator. She'd never looked back even once.

"Better make it a triple." Blanche licked her lips, her saucy grin making my stomach clench. "My boy's had a rough night, and it's about to get rougher." Did she have to wink?

I fought back a gag as Maddy paled and left our table.

"What just happened?" I asked. "I think I blacked out for a minute."

"I told that no-good tramp that you'd found greener pastures."

"Let me guess." I leaned forward and pointed at her. "Greener pastures?"

"Guilty." Another wink.

"Blanche, no offense, but I've never seen your pastures, nor do I care to."

"That's too bad. Had myself three stallions on those pastures, not one complaint."

"Were they blind? Deaf? Mute?"

"Ha!" Blanche rolled her eyes then did a little jig in her chair. "No, they were men when men were men, with callused hands and the ability to chop down any tree in the county."

"Oh good, so they won prizes in your honor? How sweet. Tell me, did they eat all the dessert at the pie-eating contest… or was that the next county fair over where you were kicked out for roughhousing with the pigs?"

Blanche straightened in her chair. "My last husband was more reckless than the first two."

"And number four? How's he doing these days?"

She grinned. "He can still stir my pot, if you get my meaning." Five more winks.

"Stop." I held up my hand. "I get your meaning without the winks, and sexual banter with you makes me want to puke into my water glass."

"So—" Blanche hacked out a cough loud enough to gain attention from people around us.

"Are you still sick?" Concern laced my words, as my stomach clenched with worry. "Did the doctor—"

"Says I'm fit as a fiddle." Blanche waved me off. "So, as I was about to say, that's the notorious Maddy, who stomped all over your heart and abandoned you, making it so that you didn't have sex for two whole years until your best friend…" Her eyes narrowed.

I sighed. "Best friend, Colt."

"Aha!" She snapped her fingers. "The best friend that got

you back on the donkey!"

"Or horse. Yeah, let's go with horse." I nodded. "Sounds better."

"But you rode a donkey."

"I rode a donkey to prove a point then ended up falling on my ass at that same college frat party, only to bump into a girl who was drunk and hot. Yes."

"Too bad you're crap in bed, huh?"

"You really need to stop reading Max's book. Nothing he says in that damn thing is even remotely true."

Damn Max for writing a bestseller on how to get women and what not to do.

Guess which part of the book I'm not in? No really. Guess.

Let's just say I had a brief moment where I thought of changing my name and moving to Canada.

"You never did tell me, is it true you gave yourself two black eyes on purpose last year so you wouldn't have to look at that girl you almost married?"

"No," I groaned. Would this day ever end? And why the hell was Max still involved in my life when he lived an hour and a half away?! Damn, it seemed the farther away I lived, the more it encouraged him to keep in touch. "Milo gave me the black eyes."

"Yes, your sister." Blanch grinned and reached for my hand again. "Which basically means you did it to yourself. What girl can hit you? You're two-hundred-twenty pounds of sirloin steak, and she's a buck-five, maybe."

"Sneak attacks. Believe me." I grunted as Maddy started making her way back to our table. "Look, can we just get our meal to go? I don't have the energy to deal with her today — or you, for that matter."

Blanche burst out laughing. "We could do things your

way…" she nodded slowly, "…or we can do them my way, and I guarantee you'll have more than enough energy by the time the night is through."

"No." I shook my head. "No, no, no! Whatever plan you have up there, you need to abort."

Blanche giggled.

"Abort!" I hissed. "Abort!"

"So, Jason," Blanche said loudly, "tell me, how do you do that trick with your tongue? Is it a secret? The girl down the street was asking me about it, and I said my escort was too classy to tell any of his trade secrets."

Holy. Hell. I rue the day I showed Blanche how to use Netflix.

chapter five

"Winning is for winners. Losing is for losers. Simple concept, but many actually fail to understand the logistics. Take, for example, my friend Jason. He looks like a winner, talks like a winner, even acts like a winner — most of the time, when he's not sporting black eyes and limps — but he's actually a loser. And this, men, is where you pay attention. He's a loser because if say... a certain past came back to haunt him, he'd open his arms and proclaim, "Welcome home! I've been waiting." Men, we don't wait. Ever. And if you are waiting, go look in the mirror, and say after me, "I will not pull a Jason," and repeat. Feel better? Good. Now go get your woman and stop crying during ESPN. It's pathetic."

~From Max Emory's Guide to Dating and Other Important Life Lessons

Maddy

ESCORT? WHAT? HE fought crime during the day as a police officer and then at night thought, “Hey, why not get more use out of those steel handcuffs?”

I tripped as the elderly lady lifted Jason’s hand into the air then kissed his palm… ending it with a good lick.

Like an ice cream cone.

He looked stunned. But maybe that was part of his gig that he playacted to their fantasies?

“Crown Royal on the rocks.” I set down their drinks and tried to appear calm, even when the lady reached into her whiskey, fished the cherry out of her glass, and held the stem between her teeth.

Jason stared at her, then at the cherry, then at me.

The woman cleared her throat.

Jason, very slowly and methodically, stood and hovered over the table, his hands pressing on either side of her plate as his head bent down. He gripped the cherry between his teeth and gave a little tug.

And I felt that stupid tug all the way down to my toes, as a shiver wracked my body.

He’d always had an amazing mouth.

A mouth that did very dangerous things, that made girls forget about things they needed to remember.

“I love it when you do that,” the lady sighed.

"And I love..." he stalled, then grinned wickedly, "pleasing you. And apparently everyone else on Main Street."

I coughed wildly, choking on my spit then cleared my throat.

"Oh." The lady sniffed in my direction.

I fought the urge to sniff myself to make sure I didn't smell.

"It's still here."

"It," I said with clenched teeth, "would like to take your order."

"Dessert," Jason piped up. "Two chocolate soufflés to go."

"Oh, Jason." She blushed. "How you tease."

"Anything else?" I just wanted to leave. This was not the Jason I'd left; then again, maybe this was the new Jason, the Jason that I'd created because of my own stupidity.

His green eyes briefly met mine. Emotion clogged my throat all over again, as I tried to keep myself from checking him out. He was huge, like MMA fighter huge, with muscles ready to burst out of his black button-up. One dimple — the dimple that made almost every female in our high school swoon against their locker — appeared. "No, Maddy, that will be all."

Dismissed.

I hurried back to the kitchen, grabbed the stupid soufflés, and stomped back to the table with their check.

"I got this, pumpkin sauce." The lady laid down a hundred-dollar bill and then eyed me. "Keep the change. After all, I think I owe you a thank you."

"Pardon?"

"Had you actually stayed with our Jason, I wouldn't have ever been privileged to experience what he has to offer. And honey, this man just gets better with time."

"Okay, we should get you in bed." Jason shot out of his chair.

The lady turned on her heel and glanced at me with a sad, yet dismissive, look. "It's a pity."

"What is?" I just had to ask.

"Knowing what he used to be like, wondering how it could get any better, and then realizing you'll never know." She smirked, grabbed the box, and whispered, "Have a good night."

chapter six

"Life isn't like a box of chocolates. Life is more like a cereal box full of grenades. You pick the colors you want and hope they don't explode before you have a chance to check the pin. But once you do, the relief and joy in that moment is incomparable because you're suddenly the most alive you've ever been. Almost scary how much sense it makes, isn't it?"

~From Max Emory's Guide to Dating and Other Important Life Lessons

Jason

"So, SOMETHING YOU need to tell me? Your best friend and confidant?" Colt set a large coffee on my desk and waited, arms crossed, stupid grin on his firefighting face.

"Suck. Ass," I replied, lifting my coffee to my lips and trying to block out the memories from the night before. Curly hair, red lips — damn it! "And no, nothing to tell."

To say I'd slept like shit the night before would be a grave understatement. From my disastrous dinner with Blanche — I'd spent the better part of the night tossing and turning, aching with need, and waking up to find myself in a cold sweat — to hunting down more signs at six in the morning. Because Max, after our conversation, had decided to double his efforts within the last twelve hours. The guy was an enigma, that was for sure.

A bored enigma.

"Interesting." The chair creaked as he leaned forward. "Because word on the street is that you were seen last night with Blanche—"

"Hardly a crime. She's nice."

"She smells like Windex, but sure..." Colton drew out sure with a judgmental tone I hated, but was used to. "And then you had a run in with—" He coughed.

"Really? Are we in high school again?" I tapped my fingers against the keyboard in an effort to ignore him. "And don't you have fires to fight? Kittens to rescue?"

"People to shame," he added with a wink. "So, Maddy's back in town." He grabbed a piece of paper and swiped one of my pencils. "How does that make you feel, exactly?"

I grit my teeth. It was bad enough when I had to deal with Max's stupid signs all over the town, but it was worse when people knew my business and watched my every move like I was a walking Netflix original. I prayed for someone to rob the bank so I'd have a reason to leave.

"It makes me feel just fine," I answered with a shaky breath. I wiped my face with my hands. "Can we not talk about this? Ever?"

"She was your only love," Colt pointed out thoughtfully.

I eyed my sidearm and wondered how much damage I could do to his right bicep if I skimmed the bullet a bit.

"First sex." This part was said loud enough to gain the attention of the chief, and at least three other officers, who all snickered to themselves.

"Get it out!" I spread my arms wide to anyone who would listen. "Yes, she was my first everything, and now she's nothing to me, you hear me? Nothing!"

The room fell quiet.

The front door of the police station closed.

And wouldn't you know?

There stood Maddy. Holding a freaking sign that said, '*Vote Max. I'm only running because I wanted to make a sign.*'

Hell, at this rate, he was going to get voted president and create a national holiday where everyone had to walk around without pants.

Cheeks flushed, she quietly dropped the sign onto the front desk and addressed our receptionist, Darla. "I have a dozen more in my car. They were all over my front yard this morning."

Darla glared at me over her shoulder as if it was my fault Max wasn't in prison and was free to actually make signs. She shook her head. "We're currently dealing with the problem. Go ahead and talk to Officer Caro. Maybe more information will stop this psychopath from littering the city," she grumbled. And then, "Should have never let that man step foot in this town."

I could have sworn Chief said, *"Amen."*

"And that's my cue." Colt waved me off. "After all, I have kittens to save."

The bastard abandoned me to Maddy.

Gorgeous, curly-haired, blue-eyed, Maddy.

Whenever I'd envisioned seeing her again, which was more often than I'd like to admit, I always pictured myself winning.

I had a secure job that paid me well; I'd already had two promotions at twenty-seven, was the most fit I'd ever been — thanks to my lack of sleep lately — and I still had all my hair and teeth.

Bonus for me.

But Maddy?

She won by simply existing.

Her bouncy hair was like a breath of fresh air in that dim police station. Her small white teeth bit down on her bottom lip, as her blue eyes raked me over with skepticism.

She was wearing black yoga tights and a tank top that said, "*Will work out for wine.*"

"Have a seat," I said, voice hoarse.

She pulled out a chair, just as I grabbed my pad and pen. The silence in the office was deafening as if everyone was waiting for me to do something stupid.

I drummed my fingertips against the table then abruptly stood. "Why don't we do this over coffee down the street? I'm fresh out, and if I have to sit and take notes about more damn signs, I'm going to lose it."

She opened her mouth, probably to object, but I wasn't used to rejection.

Not really.

The only woman who'd ever accomplished it was most likely hell-bent on doing it again. This time I wasn't going to let her. It was just coffee.

I marched toward the door.

Thankfully, she followed.

Side by side, we walked down the street. The summer air felt oddly brisk, and the wind picked up enough to sting my cheeks. *I should offer her a coat.*

But I'd left it at the office.

And I wasn't feeling very giving in that moment.

The last time I'd seen this woman, she'd rejected me.

Rejected us.

Our future.

More silence as we walked to the local Moxie Coffee. I put in my order and looked down at her.

She ordered a black coffee.

I paid for both and then sat down.

Again, she followed.

I wasn't used to her being this silent.

Things between us had been anything but.

We'd gotten detention so many times in high school for being *anything but,* that eventually they just started sending us together, mainly because we were always talking and joking around. It drove our teachers crazy, even though I was sure they'd thought it was cute that we were so close.

It was rare to fall in love with your best friend and next-door neighbor at the age of eight and then propose to her on the day of your high school graduation.

But she is it for me.

Always has been.

Always will be. Damn it.

I shoved the thoughts aside and tried again. "Address?"

She hesitated, causing me to look up.

"Um…" she tucked some of her curly hair behind her ear, "…you really don't remember?"

"It's been close to ten years," I said dryly. "How would I know where you live?"

"Because I live across the street from your parents' old house."

I nearly choked.

My parents' old place? Where I was currently staying, and remodeling, while they vacationed in Arizona for three months.

"Right." I jotted down her address by heart. "So, they were on your parents' lawn?"

Her teeth clenched. "Yes."

"Twelve, you say?"

"Yes."

"Were they placed in any intricate design?"

Her brows furrowed. "What do you mean?"

"Circles, squares, penises—"

"You're kidding."

"I wish," I grumbled. My chest felt tight, my coffee was too hot, and my uniform was beginning to itch. "So, any designs?"

"No design," she said in a small voice. "I mean, there could have been. I wasn't really paying attention. One of the signs did have one of those flyers about Spring Reunion Weekend, but that was it."

Spring Reunion Weekend.

I shuddered.

I planned on being knee-deep in sawdust during that hellish weekend, where every happy couple from high school showed off their rings, cars, babies— No, thank you.

"All right." I scribbled down more information. "I guess that's it."

She nodded slowly. "I guess it is."

Our gazes locked.

I didn't want to feel attracted to her, but it was impossible not to. She was more beautiful than the day she'd left. I tried to hold onto my hurt, but instead of building more hate, all I kept thinking was, *How is it possible that she's prettier?*

"You look good, Jason." She stood and grabbed her coffee cup. "It was..." her eyes glanced away, "...it was nice talking to you."

Bullshit. That wasn't talking, that was a painful blast from the past.

I forced myself to stay calm even though my heart was racing to run after her, tell her that I still felt... What for her?

Love?

Possibly.

Or maybe it was just a shit-ton of regret.

And pain.

That it had been so easy for her to leave me.

When I still wasn't capable of giving my heart to anyone else but the person who'd run away with it.

"Let me know if you get any more signs, all right?" Was what I said, when my mind screamed to tell her I'd missed her, to ask her why, to beg her to apologize, to see where this could lead us, to ask why she was back in New Haven.

"Yup." She waved and walked away.

The motion was so familiar.

The sight of her back.

The way she braced herself against the wind.

It was what haunted me at night.

The way she held herself so royally, while breaking my fucking heart.

chapter seven

"When faced with the Ghost of Christmas Past, your best bet is to just nod your head, smile, and apologize. Always apologize, because everyone has a past, and about 99% of us, upon reflection, should realize we're in a shitty position because of the shitty choices we made back then. So yeah, you apologize, and then you look toward your future. And if that doesn't work, you day drink."

~From Max Emory's Guide to Dating and Other Important Life Lessons

Maddy

"Well, that was painful," I grumbled over the phone to Liza.

"Don't be dramatic. I'm sure it was fine. Looks good, doesn't he? I'd lick his biceps if he'd let me."

I rolled my eyes. "Apparently, he only dates the elderly now." I thought back to last night and the woman who looked like she couldn't wait to get him home for dessert. Not only had he grown into his good looks in a way that gave normal women heart palpitations — but his intense gaze was still the same, always the same, as if he could see the depths of your soul.

The only thing missing had been a smile.

I swallowed the knot in my throat when I realized he hadn't even really made eye contact; I may as well have been invisible.

And the crappy part was, I deserved it — and more.

She choked out a laugh. "The rumors aren't true. He's just a do-gooder. He's not really prostituting himself out to Blanche, or any other old woman for that matter."

I wasn't so sure.

His stone-cold expression hadn't cracked once.

No regret had filled his eyes.

All business.

I bit down on my lip and jerked open the door to my

Ford Focus, a gift once I'd graduated college. I sighed. Four years and a hundred grand later, and what did I have to show for it?

A waitressing job.

And a degree I no longer wanted to use.

I'd hated it.

Hated living in the city.

Hated the noise.

And the fact that it was nearly impossible to make it work on such a low starting salary as an editor.

I'd shared a small apartment, rented out what looked like a closet, paid out over two grand a month for the stupid space, and barely had any money left over to do anything else by the time I paid for surviving. So, when the publisher I worked for went under…

I had no savings.

Nothing.

Nothing to help those I loved most. My chest squeezed.

I was forced to move into my old bedroom, the same bedroom that had band posters and old pictures of Jason and me.

It was like living in an actual Hell of all the reminders of why I'd left in the first place — and whom I'd left behind.

"You still there?" Liza whispered. "Either you blacked out, or I was talking to myself for a solid four minutes while you stared at the police station. Oh no, tell me you aren't standing outside his work and stalking him."

I started my car. "I'm not outside staring at the police station, just… thinking."

She whistled. "Well, can you think out loud so I know what's going on?"

"He hates me." There. I'd said it.

She huffed. "He doesn't hate you. He's just… bitter."

"Bitter," I repeated with an exhale. "Well, he has reason to be."

"You left with his best friend — with my asshole brother — the day after he asked you to marry him."

"Yeah…" Where was wine when I needed it? "But it's been ten years, and let's not forget that in that time, he got engaged and almost married—"

"Don't say it. Don't say her name. It gives me hives."

I shuddered. "Remember her in high school?"

"I try not to think about her or high school — that, too, gives me hives."

"She was the worst," I admitted. "Seriously the worst. So passive-aggressive and just… Ugh, the fact he even dated someone that selfish and crazy is just… wow

"Trick pregnancy nails those hometown boys fast," Liza said, just as a cry sounded in the background. "Gotta go. Number two's up."

The woman numbered her children. I grinned, said my goodbye, and tried not to look at the police station as I drove by; just like I tried not to stare at his parents' house when I pulled into the driveway and turned off the engine.

So many memories filled the space between our homes.

It was unfair.

My mom opened the front door and waved at me with an oven mitt.

Everything was the same.

And yet.

Everything had changed.

chapter eight

"Sometimes, the best moments in life are counted by the number of steps you take in the wrong direction. Trust me. My friend, Jason, has been walking in the wrong direction a long-ass time. Last time I counted his wrong steps, I fell asleep. The point is this, his bad choices remind me to make good choices. What else is friendship for? Count your friends' mistakes — and consider yourself lucky they aren't yours. Oh... and his name is Jason Caro. Check the spelling and check out his Instagram. Dude's like one more failed relationship away from buying a house full of cats and just sitting in his sadness."

~From Max Emory's Guide to Dating and Other Important Life Lessons

Jason

He was back.

I wasn't sure how I could tell, or the exact moment I knew it. Maybe it was when my balls tingled, when a cold sweat started to break out on my forehead, or, possibly, when I tried to get into my truck only to see that someone had deposited another fifty signs in the back.

But my body knew.

The universe was screwed.

And so was the town of New Haven.

"I've been watching you," Max said from behind me.

I looked up to the sky and prayed for a lightning bolt.

Thunder.

A bee.

At this point, I would take anything.

Slowly, I turned. "Max."

"Jason." He grinned.

I hated how good-looking the guy was. I hated how many women fell all over themselves because they thought he was hilarious and hot. And I really despised how his rabid fans had been nothing but encouraged by his damn book and tweets.

The amount of dating advice that had been sent to me via the internet from his helpful fans was alarming.

I'd changed my email at least once every two months.

And my cell number.

Well, let's just say each time Max discovered the new number, he felt the need to tweet it into the universe.

He was *"doing me a favor,"* you see.

By trying to help me, *"find a woman."*

"Impregnate her."

And, *"live on a farm."*

His words.

His plans.

The man needed a keeper.

You want to see what money and boredom do to someone? Look no further than Max Emory.

"What do you want?" I crossed my arms and waited.

He was wearing jeans and a t-shirt, a rarity from his usual business attire while running his empire from the city.

"World domination," his answer.

"You any closer than last week?"

He just shrugged. "I'm optimistic."

"How's Reid."

"Still famous."

"And you?"

He grinned. "Still rich. Hey, I get voted mayor yet?"

"First off—" I jabbed my finger into his chest. "—stop putting signs in peoples' yards before I arrest you. Second, the chief said you step foot into his town again, and he's throwing you in prison—"

"I'm too pretty for prison."

"I'll rough you up a bit to make sure you don't become someone's bitch. How's that sound?"

He nodded with a grin. "Somewhat exciting and violent. I may take you up on that. I've never been roughed-up by a cop before. Oh look, a gun. Can I hold it?"

I squeezed my eyes shut and prayed for patience. "Again, what do you want?"

He opened his mouth, but before he could get anything out, I interrupted. "Other than world domination and a house built out of Oreos."

He frowned. "It's Nutter Butters, dumbass, and I'm here for the reunion."

"My reunion?"

"Duh." He said it like I should know his reasons for attending a reunion he hadn't even been invited to. "I thought you might need a wingman."

I snorted out a laugh. "You're the worst wingman in the world. If I need a wingman, I'll grab Reid or Colt. The last time you tried to be my wingman, I ended up passed out in the dessert with a padded bra on and no recollection of the night before other than lipstick stains around my—"

"I'm hurt! You said that was the best night of your life!"

"I was drunk! And I think you drugged me. Either way, you gave out my phone number to at least fifteen strippers, all of who text me, to this day, to make sure I don't need any more help getting it up."

Max just grinned. "I told them you had limp dick from trying to shoot a spider that had invaded your house, but because your dick was blocking the way, you hit it instead. It's a compliment. Not many people can brag about hitting their own dick while trying to point and shoot!"

I started sweating immediately. "Max, I'm only going to say this one more time. Go home."

"Home is where the heart is." He grinned. "And my heart feels so warm and comfy… here. Plus, Becca's family lives here, and it's so close to the Fourth of July… why not roast some dogs? Shoot the shit?"

"One day."

"What?"

"One day, before you end up in prison."

Max chuckled, then walked around the side of my truck. "Have a little faith. Let's go."

Why is he getting in my truck?

"Max," I growled.

"What?" His innocent expression was starting to give me heartburn. "I let Becca take my car to spa day with her mom. Aren't you happy I cleared my schedule for you?"

"Thrilled," I said through clenched teeth. "But I'm on the clock, so I can't entertain you. Go exist somewhere else, like Starbucks or something!"

"Can't." His face fell. "I'm banned."

"There's more than one Starbucks."

"Oh, I meant I'm banned from all of them." He just shrugged. "Can we get a cop car and turn on the siren?"

I got in the truck and slammed the door shut. "No."

"Can we go on a chase?"

"No."

My head throbbed.

"Embark on an exciting sting operation? Shoot some caps into some asses?" He looked absolutely pumped about the idea.

"*We*..." I said the word with disdain, "...won't be doing anything. I'm dropping you off at the house and forcing you into slave labor; then I'm working for at least four more hours. Hopefully by then, your wife will be back."

"About that..." Max examined his hands. "They're gone for the weekend so..."

I started the engine and peeled out of my parking spot so fast I nearly took out Blanche who was crossing the street with one of her friends. She looked briefly at my truck and flipped me off then blew me a kiss.

Max frowned. "Silver fox. I dig it. Where you been hiding her?"

"Not. Another. Word." I hissed out, already exhausted from how much he talked.

Silence was not in Max's vocabulary. Once, he went to the library and found every dictionary in order to cross out the very word. He literally didn't acknowledge it as part of the English language.

Hello, pounding headache.

Goodbye, peaceful life.

It wasn't until I was back at my parents' house, dropping Max off, that my chest started to tighten even more.

Because there she was.

In the backyard.

Our backyard.

Playing with a water gun and giggling.

With a familiar looking little girl.

My gut clenched.

She had the same reddish-blond curls.

Same smile.

I closed my eyes.

"You okay?" Max followed my line of site and was actually quiet for a good three seconds before saying, "You didn't tell me you had a daughter."

"OUT!" I roared.

For once in his miserable life, Max listened. He hopped out of the truck and made his way into the empty house, while I gripped the steering wheel behind two sweaty hands and watched the girl play.

chapter nine

"The only true way to gain the upper hand — is to take it. I mean, that's what hands are for, right? Taking? Shaking? What the hell have you been doing the whole time? Oh I see, you were waiting for an invitation, weren't you? Sigh.

~From Max Emory's Guide to Dating and Other Important Life Lessons

Maddy

"Hey." I walked into the kitchen where my mom was currently baking bread and humming to her self.

Her hair had streaks of grey through the blond, giving it a silver hue when she moved into the light. Her lips pressed against each other then rubbed as if she was trying to figure out a problem, all before she dumped more flour onto the dough she was kneading.

"Is Dad home yet?"

"Working late again," Mom said without looking up from her masterpiece. "We'll just eat later, okay?"

I gave her a silent nod.

Then exhaled.

Then did it again.

Until, finally, she glanced up at me and smiled. "Did you need something else?"

"I saw Jason Caro."

"You mean, last night?" She stopped kneading altogether.

I had her full attention, probably because Jason had been like a son to her. When I left him, a part of her had broken too, because I was choosing the opposite of what she, and the rest of the town, had planned.

Yet another reason to run.

When you weren't in control of your own life, it seemed like the safer option to run in the opposite direction of what was killing you — and pray it wasn't too late to be saved.

"This morning..." I stared at the little specks of flour, wondering how long it would take to count them, and if it would calm me down more than the nice long jog I had planned before work. "...at the police station."

"Why were you at the police station?"

"We had weird signs in our yard, and it's been on the news that you need to report them. Some sort of stupid high school prank. I thought I was just dropping them off and then found out he's heading the whole thing and..." *One thing led to another, he hates me, ignored me for the most part, and looks like a sex god. No big deal.* "...anyway, I saw him. That's all."

"I see." She rounded the table and crossed her arms. "Do you still have... feelings for him?"

I rolled my eyes. "Mom, it was over ten years ago."

"Right." She winked. "Oh, and this came in the mail for you. You should go."

I knew what it was.

I'd been getting them every month leading up to July.

High School Reunion Weekend. Starting the very next day. They even had a Slip N Slide.

Hard pass.

The last thing I wanted to do was go to my reunion a total failure, while everyone else had a house, new cars — families to call their own.

A giggle hit my ears and then another, as the back door opened, and Anabelle ran through. "You're home!"

I gathered her into my arms and kissed the top of her curly head. "Of course, I couldn't miss out on the water gun fight!

She burst out laughing then wrapped her scraggly arms

around my neck. "You always keep your promises."

My heart clenched as I looked over her small frame to my mom, while she wiped a tear from her eye and continued making her bread.

"I try," I whispered, all the while thinking, *I try and I fail. All I do is fail, especially when it comes to Ana.* "Come on, let's go get your swimsuit on."

"Yay!" she squealed, whizzing past me and up the stairs.

Suddenly feeling older than my twenty-seven years, I took the stairs slowly, memories of making out with Jason on the third one haunting me. The creak on the tenth one was a reminder of all the times he'd tried to sneak back out the front door after spending the night.

And then the top landing where he'd stopped so often to pull me in for a kiss before descending.

Ten years, and I was a shell of my former self.

Ten years, and the hungry taste of his mouth still haunted me.

"You coming?" Ana called from inside her room.

I took a deep breath and pasted a smile on my face the same way I'd been doing since I drove away from him and left my heart on his front porch.

chapter ten

"You'll know the universe is at odds with you when you turn out like Jason. When birds shit on you and nothing else around you. When ladders collapse, cracks really do break your back, and a thundercloud follows you around for a day (swear on clouds everywhere, this actually happened; the local meteorologist quit after not being able to figure out how or why). Maybe if these things start happening... you're doing life wrong? Hell you're doing it all wrong if you've got a freaking thundercloud over your head for twenty-four hours, and experts scratch their heads."

~From Max Emory's Guide to Dating and Other Important Life Lessons

Jason

IT TOOK FIVE seconds for the universe to kick back into gear. It seemed whenever I was around Max — or my sister, for that matter — something happened to my molecular structure.

Every cell in my body shook with terror — in preparation for the other shoe to drop.

Somehow Max and Milo had turned into a curse to my body; I rarely escaped one of them without some kind of bodily harm.

And when they were together?

It was as if my body almost completely shut down right along with my brain. Maybe it was a self-defense mechanism. Maybe they both really were cursed, but I knew it was going to be a long four hours.

And that, at the end of it, I wouldn't be surprised to end up in the hospital. They knew me by first name there, not because I was a well-known cop, or even because it was a small town.

No, they'd known me by first name after the fifth Max incident. The one where he glued my hand to my penis while I was passed out.

Gorilla Glue is not meant to adhere to skin, especially skin that was used to more… sensitive loving.

My balls tingled.

Shit.

I was going to end up dead one of these days.

It had taken forever to outlive the, *"Oh hey, you're Dickhand!"*

The name Max had given me the minute they checked me in.

And since it was Max…

It had stuck.

Right along with my left hand.

I turned down the street and slammed on my brakes as a cat tried to cross the road. The liquid from my morning coffee somehow sloshed out of the cup — even though there was a lid — and went flying into my face.

Cold. Wet. Coffee.

I closed my eyes briefly, grabbed a napkin from my console, and wiped my face, then tossed it into the empty seat next to me.

The coffee spill was just a coincidence.

I pulled into my usual parking spot on the street outside the department and opened my truck door. Just then, a bus honked in my direction. I leapt back onto my seat and watched in horror as my mirror and door were amputated.

The bus driver flipped me off in the rearview mirror.

"Unbelievable!" I roared. My door was gone. MY DOOR!

At least I wasn't injured.

It could be worse.

This… this was just bad luck mixed with fleeting thoughts of a girl with bouncy curls and the one who'd birthed *her*.

Had he slept with her, then?

And later dumped her?

I bit down hard on my lip as I walked into the station.

People waved and nodded as I weaved my way to my desk and plopped down. I had scooted toward my desk when the legs on my chair somehow gave out, dropping me to the floor like a bag of bricks.

I sat in my own disappointment and annoyance for a solid minute before standing up and kicking the broken chair away. "Piece of shit."

"Maybe cut back on the donuts." Mendoza grinned as he took a huge bite of his sub sandwich.

I glared. "Did you do this?"

"Funny as hell, but sadly, no. Though, we did have a chair guy come by while you were gone. Said the chairs needed to be checked."

I stared. He couldn't be that dumb. "A chair guy? Since when have we ever needed a chair guy?"

"He's legit. I looked him up."

This was the problem with technology. Max, in all his boredom, could build a fake website in seconds. Hell, he probably did it with his phone behind his back while Mendoza questioned his legitimacy.

I paced around my desk, irrationally angry and extremely paranoid that if I opened any drawer, something was going to jump out at me; or worse, that Max had found a way to shrink himself into mini Maxes and packed them into my drawer in order to stop my heart.

Because it would.

Multiple Maxes would straight-up kill me dead.

You'd find my body on the floor, face frozen in terror as if that chick on *The Ring* had just crawled out of the TV and tried to lick my face.

"You're jumpy." Mendoza took another huge bite out of the sub, mayo spotting the corner of his mouth. "More jumpy than normal."

"I have a menace on the loose," I said under my breath. "Color me normal."

"Menace? Who?"

"Don't worry about it." *Seriously, don't.* The more I thought about him, it seemed the more the universe took control.

I very calmly walked back around to my desk, pushed my chair out of the way, and grabbed my empty coffee mug — only it wasn't empty like I thought; instead, it tsunamied over the brim and seared my hand so hard I yelped and dropped it on the floor.

"This isn't your day, man. Go home." Mendoza looked concerned, as I held my hand and swore. "I think the chair guy freshened everyone's coffee. Nice guy."

"So. Nice." I clenched my teeth and my still-burning burned hand. "I think I will take the afternoon off. Call me in if you need to."

Mendoza gave me a two-finger salute as I calmly walked out the door, holding my hand together as the fires of hell burned around my fingertips. *Just how hot was that coffee?* I made it to my truck, the one missing the door, and kicked the tire over and over again, until, with one last wallop, I led with the top of my foot, rather than the heel or point.

Something crunched.

It wasn't Max eating Pringles behind me.

It was my toe…

Dying a slow painful death as it swelled inside my boot.

"Could this day get any worse?!" I yelled. Just then, fierce rain began to fall to the cadence of thunder booming in the clouds. "Never mind."

I jumped into my truck, started it, and suffered through

ten minutes of extreme paranoia — not to mention pain — as I made my way back to the house.

I killed the engine and winced as my toe continued to throb. I needed to pull off my boot and see the damage, but the thought of looking at blood had me queasy. I limped toward the house and then paused, hearing laughter.

Of the Max variety.

It was coming from the neighbors'.

Dread pounded into my soul as feminine mirth joined with Max, and then I closed my eyes, as the pain seemed to increase tenfold.

"Jason!" Max called. "You said four hours! It's barely been one!"

"You can count," I said without turning around. "Shocked."

"I'm ignoring that insult!" Max yelled. "It wasn't even a good one. You're losing your touch, Jason."

I gave my head a shake and kept limping.

"Holy shit, what did you do?" His voice was closer.

Footsteps sounded.

And then I realized my fate. I was too injured to run to the door and lock it behind me, making me officially the baby turtle crawling across the sand toward the ocean.

And Max?

The giant dumbass bird was seconds away from sweeping my shell away and devouring me whole.

"Hey, wait a minute." Max grabbed my shoulder and flipped me around.

I let him, because fighting just seemed like another way to somehow get hurt, and with my current luck, I could see myself flailing backward and becoming concussed across the gravel by the one rock big enough to do any bodily harm.

"Did you get shot?" He frowned down at my foot.

Maddy and the little girl followed behind Max a few feet, but kept somewhat of a distance.

There may as well be a chasm between us.

"I didn't get shot," I grumbled.

Max's eyes narrowed. "So then, why are you limping?"

"People limp," I said defensively.

"Old people with arthritis, maybe. And though you are getting up there in age…"

I glared.

He just kept talking. "…I highly doubt it's because you have arthritis in your foot. Well, let's have a look." He snapped his fingers.

I glanced around me. "What do you mean, let's have a look?"

Max actually looked offended. "I'm going to see if you sprained your foot. It's what best friends do."

"You're not my best friend."

"You say that all the time, and why? We're spending the weekend together!"

My ears started to ring. "I'm sorry. Did you say *weekend?*"

"Didn't I mention that before? The whole spa thing is for the weekend, some sort of girls' trip. Milo and Jordan went too, so it's just us guys."

"Us. Guys," I repeated. "You, me—"

A Town Car pulled up to the house.

Reid and Colt jumped out and made their way toward us.

I blinked. "Max…"

"Take off the damn boot already!" He gave me a little shove. "I want to see what we're working with."

"*We're* working with nothing. *You* aren't a doctor."

"No, but he played one at drama camp one time," Reid felt the need to say.

I sent him a seething look that did nothing to force him to back down; if anything, it was as if my anger encouraged Emorys, no matter which one.

"What's wrong with his foot?" said Reid.

"Why even ask? It's Jason we're talking about here. He gets injured by breathing." Colt chuckled.

I grit my teeth. "That was one time, and the doctor said it could happen to anyone!"

"I Googled it," Max said helpfully. "It happens to llamas and those dodo birds, the really stupid ones."

I squeezed my eyes shut and prayed for patience.

"You get shot?" Reid asked.

I shoved Max away and started limping toward the door. "You guys can stay with Colt. Consider this house closed to visitors."

"Actually..." Colt cleared his throat. "—my parents said no."

I hung my head. "What are you? Twelve? You asked your parents?"

"They said last time Max—"

"Hey! Your mom enjoyed that massage immensely!"

"Enough!" I yelled. "Just ENOUGH!" I spread my arms wide and turned just in time. "My damn foot feels like it's going to fall off, my truck is missing a freaking door, and I just want to lie down in silence for a few minutes! I don't care where you guys go, or what you do, just leave me the hell alone!" The moment I said it, I knew something bad was going to happen.

I didn't, however, think it would be as severe as it was.

A crackle of lightning lit up the sky.

And then, another lit up my body.

The last thing I remembered was severe pain in my right arm, and a wave pulsing through me, before I fell to the ground and looked up at my friends' shocked expressions then closed my eyes.

chapter eleven

"Dating is an awful lot like jumping off a cliff. Okay, it's worse than that. But the cool thing is, there's nothing really to be afraid of once you jump — except for the lingering fear that you timed it wrong, or you may land on glass. Yeah that would suck — but really, anxiety leading up to the big jump is always the worst part and the landing? Never as violent as it usually seems — unless you're Jason, then you can count on landing in the one shark with his mouth wide open. Poor bastard. Point is, what's the point in living, if you aren't willing to jump at least once in your life? Ask her out. Ask him out. Tell the barista she's pretty. Just do it already and stop dicking around."

~From Max Emory's Guide to Dating and Other Important Life Lessons

Maddy

It all happened so fast.

One minute, Jason was being a jackass.

And the next minute, the sky was handing him his ass.

I gasped as he fell to the ground, and every single video I'd seen in science class came crashing down around me.

People could die from cardiac arrest.

They could go blind.

My mind surged forward with all the bad things that could happen, and before I knew it, I was running toward Jason while Max hovered over him and started doing chest compressions.

"Is he okay?" *Please be okay; please be okay*. So many words were left unsaid between us, things that needed to be dealt with. I would never forgive myself if something happened. "Jason!"

He wasn't making any noises.

Max's worried expression met mine. "Can you do CPR? I think he'd rather wake up to your lips than mine. Though, tough call."

"Hurry up!" Colt yelled.

I dropped to my knees and, with shaking hands, gripped his head on either side, then pinched his nose, and breathed into his warm, sexy mouth. The feel of his stubble against my chin made my body react so violently I ended up gasping, sucking his air rather than giving.

"That's *not* CPR," Max said under his breath as he started chest compressions again.

Jason was going to die, and it would be all my fault because I was too distracted by his mouth and the hair on his face. Really?

I tried again, this time focusing on his mouth, on giving him the air he needed. Suddenly, he made a noise, and then his eyes opened.

They locked onto me like a laser beam. My mouth was inches from his before he closed his eyes again as if he'd passed out.

"Keep going!" Max yelled.

So, I leaned in again, only to have Jason wrap his arms around me. He deepened the kiss, sliding his tongue past my lower lip so fast I didn't even have time to react, except to kiss him back.

And kiss him back hard.

Jason had always been a good kisser. Where most high school boys thought the more saliva and tongue the better, Jason kept his passion in check when needed and always made me cry out for more.

Ten years, and his kiss hadn't gotten worse.

No, it had gotten better.

He was all smooth velvet, tasting me, making my body hot all over as his lips moved across mine, covering my mouth, claiming it.

And then he pulled back and smiled.

"You pulled a *Sandlot,* you sly fox." Max grinned and then looked down at Jason's injured foot. "Holy shit, we need to get you to a hospital."

Jason shook his head. "I'm fine, I swear."

"Um…" Max started gagging.

I followed his gaze and covered my mouth. Both of Jason's boots were gone, completely singed from his feet, and his big toe was pointed the wrong way and swelling so big it looked as if he'd stepped on an apple and kept it.

One of the other guys paled. I squinted to get a better look, then felt stupid. Of course Colton would be with Jason still. He was a firefighter and married to Jason's sister, and every girl was obsessed with him, except me. No I had another obsession…

The other guy was a prettier, buffer version of Max, if that was even possible. Both guys were gorgeous. And married.

Of course.

Not that I was in the market.

But after that kiss…

My loneliness had never been so apparent.

"Stay still," Max commanded Jason. "Who the hell gets struck by lightning outside his own home?" And then he shook his head and shuddered out a, "I hope it's not like this for all Jasons."

"I'm starting to believe in the curse." Colton slid his phone into his back pocket.

I was too curious not to ask. "Curse? What curse?"

"Ah, come here, little one. Let Uncle Max tell you a story."

"Say 'Uncle Max' again, and I'm shanking you," Jason threatened from the ground. He was staring up at the sky, but his eyes looked unfocused as his head lolled from side to side as if he was fighting imaginary demons. "Are unicorns real?"

"Oh, hell," Colt mumbled. "That ambulance better hurry. He may have brain damage. I don't think it hit his head, but you never know, especially if he's asking about unicorns."

"Why wouldn't he ask about unicorns?" Max said it as if it was normal. "Anyway, back to story-time."

He was a lunatic, but I liked him, and Anabelle had thought he was hilarious, so he got bonus points for being animated and showing her how to shoot the water gun perfect every time a while earlier. I was suddenly glad Annabelle had run back into the house when Jason arrived, so she could eat lunch.

"Jason, here, has disappointed the universe with his current lifestyle."

I gulped. There it was again. His *lifestyle.* Did they mean his dating of the elderly? Or was he gay now? *Aghhh… why do I even care?*

"Lifestyle," I repeated. "You mean, he's…" I didn't want to say it.

Max's face spread into a large grin. "Too bad he kisses like a miracle, am I right?"

I felt myself blush.

"He's not gay," Colton said in a bored voice. "He's just… offended Mother Nature far too long."

"How does a person do that?" I asked, as sirens sounded.

"He got off his path," Max said simply, as the ambulance pulled up. And while everyone fussed over getting Jason into the vehicle, Max held back and whispered under his breath so only I could hear. "He didn't chase the girl."

chapter twelve

"Asking a girl out is difficult, especially if you have a nervous twitch whenever you try to say your own name. My best advice is to lead with the body, follow with the words. For example, I might lean in, smile, look away shyly, reach for my drink and graze her fingertips, then blush on cue. Oh shucks, did I just touch you? And then, when she finally locks eyes on me, I drop the bomb... I'm Max Emory, and you? Works. Every. Time. Then again, it could just be because the universe freaking loves me — it's why I get to take over one day."

~From Max Emory's Guide to Dating and Other Important Life Lessons

Jason

I DREAMT OF unicorns being set on fire.

They were extremely unfriendly, and one had Max's face and a goat's tail. I jolted awake to an IV pumping me full of fluids, and something heavy on my right foot.

My brain was a bit fuzzy I remembered yelling.

Kicking the tire of my car.

Max.

And lightning.

"Son of a bitch!" I pressed my hands to my throbbing head.

Max kicked the bed with his foot as if he was afraid to reach out and touch me.

Reid and Colt walked in with Starbucks in hand and grins on their faces.

"Took quite a spill back there, slugger." Max had his sunglasses pulled low, a sucker hanging out of his mouth. "How are you feeling?"

"Like I wish I had my sidearm," I rasped, my eyes greedily searching for the thing so I could put him down.

"I touched it," Max confessed, making me groan and close my eyes.

"Don't worry," Colton added, "He was supervised, and it wasn't loaded. Took the clip out the minute he started gazing at it as if it was a steak."

"I like big guns. They remind me of my giant cock," Max announced.

The nurse chose that wonderful time to walk in and wave at Max, who just winked back at her. She grabbed my chart and then stumbled when she laid eyes on Reid. They all did. He had this... *thing* about him that made women stumble all over themselves.

Colt cleared his throat then elbowed Reid. We had taken turns reminding him not to smile too long.

"Right." She kept reading and then felt my forehead. Her hands were cold, the coolness refreshing. "You were struck by lightning, Mr. Caro. We ran tests, and the only thing that seems to be wrong with you is your toe. We bandaged it up, but there's really nothing more we can do—"

"They have to amputate," Max said seriously.

And like an idiot, I believed him.

She gave him a scolding look then tucked her dark hair behind her ear as if she was seconds away from asking him if he wanted to go get coffee, and needing to make herself more appealing by giving him her best side.

Unbelievable.

"He's kidding. Your toe's going to be just fine. Try to get some rest. You've been through a lot today."

I eyed Max. "No, really?" Sarcasm dripped off every word while I continued to stare the psycho down, but he just shrugged as if it wasn't his presence that caused the universe to hate me.

"Take today and the rest of the weekend to rest, all right? No... um... strenuous activities." Her cheeks pinked.

"Oh, that won't be a problem," Max interrupted. "He's—"

I kicked him with my good foot, shutting him up.

"I'm not currently seeing anyone," I said in a flat voice. "So, no worries. I won't be bouncing on a mattress anytime soon." The thought was so depressing I wanted to bang my head against a wall.

"Bouncing?" Reid frowned. "Who the hell bounces during sex? Are you doing the bouncing, or is she? Because, I gotta tell you, man, if you're bouncing, you've been doing it wrong."

"Thanks," I said through clenched teeth. "And I was being sarcastic."

"Sure you were." Max patted my good leg.

I swore my entire body was ready to just launch itself at him and strike wherever I could.

The nurse excused herself while I closed my eyes and leaned back against the pillows, dreaming of lips that touched mine, dreaming of making out with my high school girlfriend in the space between our houses. We'd always joked that it was our state line. And every time the chalk line between the pavement of our driveways faded, one of us would take it upon ourselves to draw it up again, step over, and ask for a kiss.

Stupid.

So stupid.

The minute she walked away, I'd grabbed a hose and sprayed away the chalk as the sting of tears burned my eyes.

We were supposed to be forever.

And then she'd turned her back on me.

I groaned. Why was I thinking of her now? She'd probably seen me get hit by lightning. No woman in her right mind would attach herself to me in my current state of chaos.

"So," Max said interrupting my thoughts, "how was that CPR?"

I felt my body weaken. "Shit, if any part of your mouth touched mine, I'm getting plastic surgery to replace my skin."

"A bit dramatic," he laughed. "And no, that was all your ex-girlfriend, the one who broke your heart—"

"I remember. Thanks," I hissed.

"The kiss?"

"The broken heart," I corrected, looking away.

"You should bring her flowers, tell her thank you for saving your pathetic life. Maybe draw her a bubble bath—"

"Don't listen to Max," Reid piped up. "Women love big gestures, you know? Write her a poem or—"

Colt burst out laughing. "Both of you shut the hell up. He needs to do something that reminds her of how good they were."

"Stop!" I raised my voice, head pounding. "I'm not thanking her, and I'm sure as hell not touching the one woman who's still capable of making me regret every decision I ever made in high school, all right? Just drop it!"

A knock sounded on the door.

And then she appeared through it, hands shaking as she held out flowers and a teddy bear.

Numb.

I felt so damn numb when her eyes met mine.

And when she glared, I was ashamed to admit my dick twitched as if it was ready to get on board with whatever sort of punishment she had, if I could only get close to that creamy skin.

"Good to know." She nodded her head. "Guess I'll just leave you alone." She deposited the flowers and teddy into Reid's hands and ran out.

Shit.

Max started slow-clapping loud enough to make me

want to cut off his hands.

I wiped my face with my palms and swore.

"He always had no game?" Reid asked Colt.

Colt stared me down. He'd been my best friend since we could talk. He was the only one who knew me better than I sometimes knew myself, and he knew, just like I did, that I was pushing her away on purpose.

Because it would be too easy to pull her close.

Too easy to risk it all over again.

Too easy to lose my heart.

Hell, who am I kidding?

She still had it.

She always would.

chapter thirteen

"Even when you're holding the shards of your own broken heart in the palm of your hands, insulting the one person responsible for the breaking isn't going to magically heal or fuse the pieces back together. The heart works as one muscle; continue to go against its one purpose — beating — and the pieces just get smaller and more jagged. I know, I know, shit just got real, but truth bombs are necessary when it comes to the heart. Don't be a jackass and make it worse."

~From Max Emory's Guide to Dating and Other Important Life Lessons

Maddy

THE BURN OF fresh tears hit me so hard and fast that I'd had to basically run from his stupid hospital room. Before the ambulance left, Max and I had exchanged numbers so he could keep me updated, and when he suggested I stop by, I'd jumped at the chance.

Because that kiss…

It felt like a promise.

It felt like maybe a fresh start.

Plus, he'd been semi-awake, right? He'd wanted it as badly as I had. Or I thought he had.

The Jason Caro I fell in love with no longer existed.

And I only had myself to blame.

My fault.

With legs like lead, I worked for the next six hours trying to smile at customers and laugh at their jokes, but I felt empty. Liza even asked if I was sick.

Sick?

Yeah, my heart was sick.

So sick and tired.

And I had all weekend to think about my bad choices and where everything had gone wrong; sadly, that memory was worn in my brain. And in every moment of weakness, when anxiety crept in, when regret filled me from head to toe, it flashed before my eyes; the day I'd ruined the best thing that had ever happened to me and thrown it away like trash.

"Marry me?" Jason was down on one knee in front of the entire graduating class.

Girls all around me were fanning themselves, giggling, wishing they were me. There were two men everyone wanted in that stupid school, Jason and his best friend, Colton. I bit down on my lower lip as our future flashed before my eyes. I wanted to go to college, and he wanted to stay local and become a police officer. Nothing wrong with that, but how could we be married and live so far away?

My sister gave me a thumbs-up in the crowd; she'd driven down from NYU just to see the proposal. It wouldn't surprise me if she'd helped Jason pick out the ring.

I nodded, my voice gone.

The minute I made the motion.

I regretted it.

Not him.

The decision.

I stared into his hypnotic green eyes and felt sick to my stomach. This man… I would break his heart, but what other option did I have? This would destroy us. Getting married so young after only ever being with each other? Starting our lives together before we even knew who we were individually?

I knew it was wrong.

And I still said yes.

I tried not to flinch when I heard a girl behind me whisper, "She's going to turn out just like her mom… another local bites the dust."

My heart fell to my knees.

"Love you, baby." Jason kissed me on the mouth. His smile

was so wide, so permanently etched across his face, that I didn't have the heart to tell him anything.

So, I waited.

I'd waited for hours.

And then I couldn't wait anymore.

A tear slid down my cheek as I finished up my shift and headed back to the house. Jason's truck was parked in its spot, and another car I didn't recognize was next to it.

I wiped my tears away and slowly made the trek toward my front door, when I heard a throat clear.

I pressed my hand to my chest and looked over my shoulder.

Jason was standing there, hands inside the pockets of his worn jeans, and an old Yankees baseball vintage tee plastered against his muscular body. "I'm sorry."

His voice was still that same gruff tenor that had every woman who knew him sighing to herself and glaring at me with envy. He wasn't just a catch, he was the catch of the town.

And I'd let him go.

Because of a few stupid comments about my mom, because of my own insecurities, because of my own fear.

I swallowed the baseball in my throat and slowly made my way over to him. A lifetime separated us, at least that was what it felt like as I walked through the wet grass toward my past.

The thick air was already feeling more like summer every day, causing perspiration to collect on my lower back. The moon was out, and streetlights flickered overhead.

"How are you feeling?" It was a safe question, one that wouldn't acknowledge that he basically hated me.

His lips twitched. "Oh, you know, like I got struck by lightning."

I covered my mouth with my hand and tried to keep my laugh in. It really wasn't funny.

Not funny.

Not funny.

Not funny.

He full-on grinned.

Causing me to burst out laughing.

I covered my mouth with my hands again and whispered through my fingers, "I'm so sorry. It's just… only you."

"Yeah…" he rocked back on his heels, "…only me. Look…" He pulled his hands out of his pocket and took a step forward, his toe coming into contact with the invisible chalk barrier we used to put up between our houses. "…I'm a jackass. I really have no other reason for the things I do or say when it comes to you. Nobody deserves to be treated that way, so yeah, I'm sorry."

"Sorry that I heard you, or sorry that you said it?" Where had that brave question come from? *A time machine would be extremely handy right about now.*

His eyes widened a bit before he blew out a breath and looked down at the cement. "A bit of both, actually."

"Honesty." God, it felt like he'd stabbed me in the heart, and the worst part was that I deserved it.

"Aunt Maddy! Aunt Maddy!" Annabelle came running out of the house and down the stairs. She crossed the lawn with such relentless joy that my heart cracked even further. "I lost a tooth!"

"Whoa!" I held out my hand for a high-five then pulled her in for a hug.

Jason looked between us; dawning lit up his face and

then… the worst emotion, the one I didn't want to see.

Relief.

He looked relieved, which just pissed me off more.

"Aunt," he said with a smile on his face. "Is Sara visiting too, then?"

Annabelle tightened her hold on my hand and then wrapped her scrawny arms around my waist.

"Go back inside, Ana. I'll be in soon, okay?" I kissed her on the head while she nodded and ran back into the house.

The minute the door shut, I unleashed. "Do you really think I would hide a kid from you? Especially if it was yours?"

"It could have been his too," his response.

"You really are a jackass!" I screamed, shoving him backward toward his house. The man was so built he barely moved an inch, but it still made me feel better.

He reached for me.

I jerked away.

Sighing, he hung his head. "Look, I'm sorry. Again. I just thought, maybe that's why—"

"Maybe that's why I left?" I finished for him. "I cheated on you and got knocked up by one of your friends? Did you even know me?"

"Apparently not, since it was so easy for you to jump into bed with one of my best friends then run away with him the day after breaking off our engagement."

My hand went flying.

He closed his eyes as my palm stung his left cheek.

"Shit!" I shook my hand and then held it.

"Let me see—"

"NO!" I screamed at him in outrage. "You don't get to touch me. Take your assumptions and your lit up lightning ass back to your house."

He smirked. "Still got that spunk."

"So help me God, I will run you over with your own truck, Jason. Don't tempt me!"

His eyes brightened, and then they went dark. "A little violent since I last saw you. Then again, I didn't really see your face. It was more of your tight ass as you got into his Jeep and didn't look back."

"If I'd looked back, I wouldn't have gone!" I roared. "Now leave me and my family alone." A part of me remembered that I needed to apologize, that part of my grief included building bridges that I'd broken in the past, but that part was so pissed off, it raged for justice.

"You're reminding me of your sister," he finally said. "Tell her I said, 'hi.'"

"I would," I said in a quiet voice, "if she wasn't on some bender. For all I know, she's dead."

With that, I walked back toward the house, only to hear footsteps behind me.

Jason grabbed my wrist and turned me around. "What do you mean she's on a bender?"

"I mean, she got pregnant by one of her druggie boyfriends and gave up her daughter the minute she started doing drugs again. What? Did you think I came back for you?" It was true, but he didn't need to know that. "I'm helping raise Annabelle, because Sara won't. Goodnight, Jason."

I slammed the door behind me and leaned against it. My mom and dad were both quietly sitting in the living room, pretending to be watching the news.

I groaned. "I know you heard."

"Honey…" Mom didn't take her eyes off the TV, "…the whole neighborhood heard."

Dad winced. "Weren't you a little hard on him?"

I grunted. "Not hard enough. Not by a long shot. I'm going to go read a story to Annabelle and say goodnight."

They both nodded.

And I was suddenly thankful they weren't handing out free advice, because I was in no state of mind to take it now, or maybe ever.

Damn you, Jason.

chapter fourteen

"Food and sex are the same thing. Seriously. Eating a good burger is just like having a good orgasm, I mean depending on the partner and the burger joint, duh. The point is this, when you're feeling alone in the universe, the universe provides! Might I suggest a nice juicy steak? Just remember to savor it, just like you would sex, and I promise, those little happy chemicals will get you every single time. I'm sure that's what my friend Jason does, since he's not getting any. Reference earlier chapters for correct spelling and his phone number. Oh, and I'll leave it in the author notes, just in case. Say it with me, 'STEAK SAVES LIVES!'"

~From Max Emory's Guide to Dating and Other Important Life Lessons

Jason

"KA POW!" MAX made an exploding motion with his hands as I walked into the newly refurbished living room. "That was about how good that apology went, just in case you were wondering."

"Dumbass, that's not an exploding sound, just in case *you* were wondering," I snapped back, as I limped to the nearest chair and plopped down.

Reid, Max, and Colt were all there.

And I was in Hell.

The women were gone.

So basically, I had nobody to give me good advice.

But three married men were looking at me like I was their next project, because they were so bored with their lives that they'd forgotten how to live without a female by their sides.

"So, I have an idea." Max cleared his throat.

"Last time you had an idea, Jason ended up in prison. I'd tread lightly, Obi-Wan." Colt chuckled while Reid snorted next to him. We'd all been on the receiving end of Max's ideas — we had scars to prove it — and yet, Max always came away unscathed, funny thing, that.

"No," I answered just as he opened his mouth.

He ignored me.

I knew he would.

But I needed to at least still fight and hope he tuckered himself out.

"You need closure." Max nodded like he was the wisest dating guru on the planet. *New York Times bestselling dating book be damned to the pits of Hell!*

"And you're not going to get that unless you make nice with your neighbor."

"As much as it pains me to admit…" Colt leveled me with a serious look.

"Don't say it. Please don't say it. He's hard enough to live with as it is," Reid pleaded.

"He's right," Colt said, releasing the most dangerous sentence known to mankind spiraling into the universe.

I sucked in a breath and waited for an asteroid to hit the earth.

It didn't.

Damn it.

Max leaned forward, his face suddenly serious. "You can't commit to someone new until you patch up what went wrong with Blue Eyes."

"Blue Eyes?"

"My nickname for her. Such deep blue eyes, you get lost in the depths of—"

"Feel free to punch him." Reid cleared his throat. "Jason, really, nobody would judge you. I'll even hold him down."

"I'll video," Colt offered.

Max rolled his eyes. "Perfect nickname aside, I think you guys should patch things up. Be the bigger man."

"I am the bigger man!" I roared. "She walked away from me, not the other way around! I loved her. I wanted to marry her, have kids with her. I wanted a future with her!" My chest was heaving, and by the time I was done talking, I was out of breath, staring dumbly at three married men who gave me a knowing look of pity.

God, I hated that look.

I sighed into my hands. "Every time I see her, I want to yell."

"Because you're angry," Max said matter-of-factly. "And where there's anger, the heart 'twill not grow."

"The hell?" Colt rasped. "He just say, "twill?'"

"It's a word. Look it up," Max fired back, before giving me his attention again. "Do you really want to be the guy on the force who starts rescuing cats just so he can take them home?"

"Firefighters rescue cats," I pointed out.

"Dogs, cats, goats — whatever. The point is this. You're going to start picking up strays."

"You. Don't. Say." I glared at him.

He didn't get it.

Either he refused to acknowledge that he *was* said stray, or he was an idiot, and as much as I'd like to believe the second, I knew he was more evil genius than anything.

"Friends!" Max said, like it was the most brilliant idea he'd ever had. "You guys need to hang out again, mend the broken bridges. I say you make a list of all the things you guys used to do when you were the dynamic duo." The old nickname was like a punch to the gut. "And when you're done…" he shrugged, "…at least you'll know that you can really move on, get married, find a wife who tolerates you, and get all the sex from her."

"I can get all the sex now."

"Aw…" he patted my knee, "…that's cute."

I dug my fingers into the chair and waited for some other brilliance to be suggested; instead, Colt and Reid just gave me a look of... *Well, it was worth a shot.*

Ten minutes later.

Three beers later.

And Colton had helped conjure up a list of things Maddy and I used to be notorious for.

Starting with setting the police station on fire.

"This is going to be the best guys' weekend of our lives." Max rubbed his hands together. "And just in time for the reunion this weekend, where I swear on my life, I will find you a woman who finds you attractive. You can show her your goods, and all will be well in the universe. No more accidents."

No more accidents?

The idea had merit.

And maybe I was buzzed, but the fact that I could finally put the past behind me, finally walk under a ladder without knowing it was going to fall on me...

It sounded nice.

Living.

Not getting struck by lightning sounded incredible.

It was definitely the alcohol talking, but at the end of the night, I reached over, gave Max a high-five, and said, "Let's do it."

I'm going to take a momentary time out in the story, kids. Encouraging Max is like pulling the clip from a grenade and knowing it's going to explode in your face, but holding tight anyway.

In a long list of bad ideas, this was probably the worst, but I still agreed, and I know in my gut I will regret it later.

This is a good time for you to run along and grab some popcorn, because things?

They're about to get good.

chapter fifteen

"In another life, I could have been a monk — but my body was made for performance and I heard it wasn't safe to go without sex for too long. The point? I'm basically as close to sainthood as a person can get. Want to know why? Because I see someone in need, and I help them. Need some advice? Stop looking inward, find a pathetic bastard who needs your help, and do the right thing. Well! GO!"

~From Max Emory's Guide to Dating and Other Important Life Lessons

Maddy

I FELL INTO a dreamless sleep, only to wake up when something kept smacking against my window. I grabbed the old baseball bat in the corner and slowly pulled the curtains back.

Jason was standing below, a few rocks in hand, chucking them at the glass.

I glanced back at the clock.

Four in the morning?

Really?

I jerked open the window. "What the hell are you doing? Do you know how late it is?"

"I'm drunk."

I sighed. "Of course you are."

"Max's fault."

He was still beautiful, even drunk, his biceps tightened beneath that same vintage shirt. I wanted to squeeze them. I wanted to kiss him again, to feel him on top of me, or on bottom — I wasn't picky.

He's an ass.

He's a complete ass.

But why did he have to look so good with a backward baseball cap on and a five o'clock shadow?

WHY!

"Give me two days."

"Two days? I'm confused. Is this more drunken talk, because I really need to go back to bed." I turned.

"Wait!" he yelled, probably waking up the entire neighborhood.

I made a motion with my hands. "Shh! You're going to wake up my parents."

He grinned wickedly. "Wouldn't be the first time, now would it, Maddy?"

I felt my face heat.

He'd barely escaped that night. We'd had sex in my room, and I'd been too loud. Suddenly, the lights to the hall flicked on, and Jason made a narrow escape onto the roof.

"You're blushing," he pointed out.

"No, I'm not."

"You are."

"Jason."

"Do you remember? What it felt like? Me inside you, my hands roaming all over your soft body… the way you screamed my name every time I licked your—"

"Enough." I clenched my thighs together. "I'm serious, Jason."

"Two days of friendship," he announced. "Two days without the past, only the present. Give me two days."

"Why would I do that?"

His face saddened. "For closure, for both of us…"

Closure. The word gutted me, made me want to puke in the corner then start rocking.

But I knew I needed it just as much as he did.

And since my therapist felt like it would be good for me to go home and deal with the one situation that had always plagued me…

I heard myself whispering, "Yes."

"We start in..." he checked his imaginary watch, "... three hours. Get ready, baby. Things are about to get... heated."

"I thought you said friends?"

"I mean, literally. Say a prayer I don't get fired." He winked, and then he scampered off as if we hadn't just had a yelling match a few hours earlier.

As if we didn't have a chasm of pain between us.

Like he used to, so many years ago, when he'd stand outside my window and chat with me for hours because he said he'd rather see my face in person than talk on the phone.

I closed the window, crawled back into bed, and hugged my knees. I almost hadn't survived leaving him. How in the world was I going to survive this? Doing it again? Only this time, I would be the one begging him to stay, and Jason Caro — the man I'd always loved — would be the one walking away.

Karma.

Sucked.

chapter sixteen

"Love is stupid. I hate it almost as much as I love it. Because it makes men irrational, it makes them — crazy. Almost like a perpetual drunkenness has taken over their body. Swear, I look drunk at least 98% of the time, and I blame my Becca, but have you seen her? Who wouldn't wear a dopey smile? Now, look in the mirror. If you look sober, you aren't in love. See? How hard was that? Now you know, kiddo!"

~From Max Emory's Guide to Dating and Other Important Life Lessons

Jason

"If I get fired, I'm killing you in your sleep. I'm not kidding, man. I'll even smile doing it," I warned Max.

He just gave me a blank stare and said, "Your threat is empty, just like your soul." He ended it with a hiccup then pounded his chest. "Shit, I think I'm still drunk."

"You're swaying." Reid poked him with the lighter.

Max grabbed onto the side of the house to steady himself for a couple minutes. Colt finally appeared from the front door, backpack in hand.

I narrowed my eyes. "What's that?"

"Your old backpack."

"No shit. Why do you have it?"

"You're reliving all the things, and during this time," Max announced, "you had a blue backpack, and in that blue backpack…"

"Yeah, I know..." my gut clenched, "…I kept candy, twenty-four seven, because the girl I loved was so damn sweet." *God, I was an idiot. No wonder she left me. Did I really say shit like that? Out loud? To another human? It's a miracle I ever got laid!*

"Blesses—" Max burped and pounded his chest, "—my heart."

I fanned my hand in his face. "Rum and broken promises, that's what you smell like."

"Thanks, man." He patted me on the shoulder while Colt handed me the backpack. "All right, day one of 'find your heart and stop thinking with your dick' has officially started. Go get 'em, tiger."

I started sweating immediately.

I walked up to her door with a stupid blue backpack, wearing jeans and a t-shirt like I had all through high school, and knew what I was about to subject myself to.

Last night it had sounded good.

So had a hotdog.

I should have chosen the hotdog and gone to bed. *Damn it!*

I knocked once, twice, and was about to knock a third time, when the door swung open and little Annabelle stared up at me with wide blue eyes. "You're tall."

I chuckled. "Yeah, well, you're short."

She gasped. "That's not nice."

"Why not?" I leaned down until I was hunched on the ground at eye-level. "Being short's the best. You can sneak in places tall, bulky people like me can't. I bet you're the best at hide and seek, would probably beat me every time."

She smiled so big and bright, I felt like someone had kicked me in the gut. Her toothless grin was so trusting, so innocent.

Damnit, Sara, what happened to you? I wished I could say I was surprised, but the drug problems in this country were no joke, and it could happen to anyone, even straight-A students with full rides to NYU.

"I *am* the best at hide and seek!" she confirmed, jolting my thoughts away from Sara. "Everyone says so."

"Who's everyone?"

"Papa, Grandma, Aunt Maddy."

"That's everyone that counts," I agreed.

She giggled. "Are you here for Aunt Maddy?"

"Yeah, could you run along and grab her for me?"

"She yelled at you last night."

I cringed. "She had reason to."

"You can't be mean to her," she announced with a lift of her chin, "or else I'll tell."

I loved her threat, her little protectiveness over Maddy. "I cross my heart and hope to die."

"Stick a *billion*..." she yelled the billion part, "...needles in your eye!"

"A billion, that's rough, and yes, stick a billion needles in my eye."

"Now pinky promise." She held out her tiny hand.

I linked my pinky with hers and forced a smile. Our own daughter would have looked a lot like this, the little girl I'd wanted with Maddy, the family I'd wanted to start.

Get a grip, Jason.

We released fingers just as Maddy bounded down the stairs in roughed-up black skinny jeans, Converse, and a loose-fitting white tank that hung a bit on her curvy body. She had an old blue Mets hat covering her bouncing curls, and from what I could see, minimal makeup, just the way I always remembered her — fresh, beautiful. She was the epitome of the girl next door, and she'd been mine — until she wasn't anymore.

Maddy didn't give me one second of her attention; everything was focused on Annabelle. "Make sure you brush your teeth after breakfast, and don't give Papa a hard time if he tells you to rest a bit in your room after lunch, all right?"

Annabelle sighed. "I'm too old for naps."

"You're seven. Think of it more like a happy time-out.

You can bring in four books."

"Five."

"Four."

"Six."

Maddy groaned. "Five. And not one more."

Annabelle beamed. "Thanks, Aunt Maddy. Love you." She wrapped her arms around her leg, and Maddy leaned over and kissed the top of her head.

"Love you too, munchkin."

"Have fun on your date!" she called, just as the door slammed.

Maddy turned and opened her mouth, while I grinned to myself and held out my hand.

"Remember," I said, my hand mid-air, "no ugly past, only the good parts, and the present. You ready for a good time?"

She rolled her eyes and took my hand. "That's the last thing you said to me before I got my first speeding ticket."

"And I was right. It was a good time." I shrugged.

Maddy elbowed me. "Oh yeah, it was fantastic until the cop gave me a ticket, and my dad grounded me from my own car for a month."

"Eh, my truck had more backseat space."

Her face lit up crimson.

I couldn't look away from that blush, had never been able to; something about the way she wore her feelings so apparent on her skin was such a damn turn on, I was hard as a rock every time I teased her — which was about as often as it was awkward.

As it was, I was having a hard time keeping myself in check; if my pants were any tighter, I was going to have to have a talk with my zipper and the way it kept rubbing.

I opened up my old truck door for her. The one I'd driven in high school, not the one that was currently sporting a missing door. I figured it would be best to just drive the thing and risk more injuries to something older. My parents would kill me if I ruined their new Benz. I didn't want to take the chance that the universe was still against me.

I got in on my side and fired up the engine.

It still smelled the same, like old gasoline and spearmint gum.

My eyes fell to the heart she'd drawn in permanent marker on the steering wheel with her name on it. It had been my reminder that I had special cargo next to me, and that I needed to keep it safe at all costs.

And I had.

Not one ticket.

Maddy glanced over at me. Her eyes fell to the space between us that she used to fill. I'd hated her sitting far away.

I bit down on my lip. If we were going to do this, we needed to do it right. With a sigh, I grabbed her leg and pulled her body toward the center. She came without a fight. My hands shook as I reached for the steering wheel and then her hand was on my thigh as if nothing had changed in the last decade.

When everything had.

The smell of the truck, of her, of the memories slamming into me, was almost too much. I squeezed my eyes shut and inhaled.

"Let's go," I said with a weary sigh, trying like hell not to react to her touch and trying even harder to keep my anger and resentment on hold. If she could do this, I could do this. After all, I needed to get over her, over us. I needed to see that it wasn't the same anymore. We'd grown apart. We were different people.

Closure meant I could move on. Really move on.

And I needed that more than I realized.

Because the minute I started driving down the road, my heart sprang to life in my chest. Ten years I'd been holding onto this dream of her, of us.

It was damn time to let go.

chapter seventeen

"Walking down memory lane with an old flame will do one of two things. One, it makes you remember only the good times, causing you to fall into another stupid relationship that should have always stayed in the past. Or two, it causes you to put all the shit behind you, and try again. It's fifty,-fifty. Then again, those are the odds of crossing the street right? Wrong. I was testing you. You failed. Stop nodding your head dumbass, and listen. ONLY embark with an old flame if a dating guru says it's okay. Geez, amateurs all around me. I'm getting itchy thinking about it."

~From Max Emory's Guide to Dating and Other Important Life Lessons

Maddy

IT WAS THE ultimate bad idea: stir up feelings, pretend like we didn't have all of this pain and rejection between us, and just ride into the sunset, or in my case, toward downtown as if nothing had happened in ten years, when everything had.

I blamed myself.

But I also blamed Jason.

I was angry at him for not understanding when I'd tried talking to him about it, for not getting how the logistics didn't work — wouldn't work — and I wasn't willing to risk our friendship, our love, even if he was.

I cleared my throat and tried to ignore the way my palm heated against his thigh, and how close I was to places I used to touch while he was driving; things I would do that would make me blush if I thought too hard.

How were we never caught?

Or arrested, more than twice?

It was truly a miracle.

Especially with all the shenanigans that had gone on in this truck. I knew, without a doubt, that if I slid my hand into the back pocket of the driver's side, I'd find a bag of M&Ms, just in case, right along with a box of condoms.

I swallowed and kept my eyes forward, as images of Jason peeling off his shirt and tossing it outside the truck flashed in the forefront of my mind; him unbuttoning his jeans while

I gasped into his mouth, the truck idling in the dark at the football field near the bleachers, his body hovering over mine as our mouths connected, bodies synced…

Sex with Jason had always felt right.

Not like I had done anything wrong.

Even though we'd been young…

He'd felt like my forever.

And nothing was ever awkward; it had only been perfect.

"I love you, baby," Jason sighed against my neck, his teeth grazing my skin, causing me to let out a little moan as I fumbled for the front of his jeans. His dark laugher filled the clear night air as he helped me along, and then pulled me into his lap so I was straddling him. "We don't have to rush."

"I know." I didn't tell him I was afraid of what would happen after graduation — what would happen to us. I didn't tell him I was terrified of staying, of what our lives would look like if we just stayed. I didn't want to be that person, and a part of him knew that, but we didn't talk about my fears because I didn't want him to think I didn't love him enough to stay local. "I love you."

His face relaxed as he stole another kiss.

The sound of a condom opening paired with our mouths all over each other, dying for another taste; teenage bodies aching for release far beyond their realm of understanding. He pulled my cheerleading skirt up, then dug his finger into my black Spanx. I let out a gasp as he moved me to my knees and slinked them down my thighs. I stood in the truck bed, under the stars above the football field, and looked down at his hungry green eyes. He kissed the inside of my thigh and tugged the Spanx over my knees. I gulped when they were at my feet, when I stepped out and lowered myself back onto him.

Wrapper discarded.

Just us.

Joined where he'd thrown another touchdown under the bright lights. Why couldn't it always feel like this? Just us, no harsh whispers, no judgment, just me and the boy I loved?

"You are my everything." Our foreheads touched as he made promises I wanted him to both break and keep.

I kissed away the words. I lost myself in him as he moved inside me, as the fall air reminded me time was running out. As I spotted his jersey in the bed of the truck and felt tears well in my eyes. His skin was hot to the touch, and with each slow movement, each thrust, I thought to myself.

This. Is. Perfect.

And the wind blew as I clung to him for dear life, moving with his body as we both cried out — as his name fell from my lips.

I pressed my free hand to my chest and sighed.

"You all right?" Jason grinned over at me.

He was all man now.

All. Man.

From the way his jeans molded against thick thighs that you were sure never missed leg day — ever… to the cut chin, chiseled features, and I won't even start on what that man looked like in a uniform.

"Yeah," my voice croaked. "I'm good, just… thinking."

"Stop." His smile was warm, melting me from head to toe as if I'd been shivering in the cold all this time, just waiting for him to invite me inside for hot chocolate.

Oh, this is bad. I should have never said yes. My defenses are already down after three minutes! Imagine two days!

He pulled behind the police station.

I frowned. "What are we doing at your work?"

"Ah, today I'm not a cop. I have it off, remember? Freak injury where the God of Thunder decided to strike my ass with lightning? You were there…"

I grinned, sucking my bottom lip between my teeth. "Yeah, looked rough. You screamed like a girl."

He glared. "I'm pretty sure I passed out first."

"After you pissed yourself, yup."

He gave me a shove while I laughed. "I didn't piss myself." He seemed uncertain.

I put him out of his misery. "Okay fine, you didn't, but it could have happened. Imagine your embarrassment then."

"I got struck by lightning in front of the girl who stole my heart and never gave it back. Imagine my embarrassment now."

I sucked in a breath.

He looked away. "Sorry, that was uncalled for."

"No." I reached for him, but he was out of the truck before my fingers could grasp at his tanned and toned arm. "Sorry," I said, as he shut the truck door and walked around to open mine.

By the time he did, his expression was clouded, yet he was smiling.

He grabbed the blue backpack that held almost as many memories as the damn truck, threw it over his shoulder, and motioned for me to be quiet.

My eyes narrowed.

Was he?

No, he wouldn't do that.

Couldn't he get fired? There had to be another reason we were at the police station, reliving old times, with his damn backpack.

I prayed I was wrong, when he pulled out a firecracker and held it up.

"Jason..." I warned, "...you could get fired."

"It's almost time for the first lunch break. Nobody's here, and if they are, I'll just blame it on some punk-ass high school kid who had the nerve to interrupt my brunch date."

"Did you say brunch?"

He pulled out a bag of gummy worms and then two cups of Top Ramen. "Be right back. I need some hot water."

He walked right into the back door of the station then returned with both cups steaming and a fork poking out each side.

I took my cup and grinned. "I haven't had Top Ramen since... well, since high school."

"You mean you don't often challenge your body by using up two days' worth of sodium just so you can have a noodle-fest? That's not normal." He grinned over his cup. I could almost feel it, the tether we used to have, trying to snap between us and hold tight.

And then he looked away.

And it was gone.

"I'm more of a quinoa-type of girl," I admitted.

He jerked his gaze to mine. "Please tell me you still eat meat." He looked pale.

I nodded. "Still eat—" I choked out "—meat," when my eyes accidentally fell to his crotch then back up again. *Freaking well done!*

His eyes widened before he coughed out a laugh. "Good to know you don't discriminate."

Someone shoot me.

We finished our soup in companionable silence before he grabbed a set of matches and winked at me. "You ready for this?"

"Jason, I don't—"

He lit the firecracker and tossed it into the dumpster behind the station.

The second it set off…

We ran like hell, hand in hand, to the front of the station where several cop cars were sitting.

Jason grinned then dashed into the station and right back out. He unlocked the closest car and jumped in.

I followed, my teeth chattering, as he sped off and turned on the siren.

I sunk into my seat. "Please don't tell me we just stole a cop car."

"Eh, Chief won't care."

I paled. "The chief? We stole his cruiser?"

Jason burst out laughing. "No, we stole mine, but I'm not supposed to be working, so we're still living on the dangerous side there, Candy Lips."

My heart sped up.

Candy Lips.

I'd loathed that nickname.

He'd said I tasted like candy.

It was so romantic—yet embarrassing—when he referenced it around school that I'd started calling him Candy Lips, too. His friends gave him hell; he said they were just jealous they only had their right hand and Victoria's Secret, while he possessed the real thing.

Jason accelerated. I let out a squeal as we pulled into the old high school parking lot. It was nearly empty since it was the beginning of July, and people were out of school already. Though there were a few sparse cars littered around, probably because of summer practices and camps.

"Let's see what else this magic backpack holds." He grabbed it, and we stepped out.

"Wait…" I leaned over the cop car, "…you didn't pack it?"

"Nope…" he shrugged. "This backpack is the result of too much beer, followed by whiskey and a few shots of tequila, unmanly confessions, and Colt's big fat mouth."

"Oh great…" I laughed. "He has enough dirt on both of us to make me nervous."

Jason snorted. "And yet he's been sitting on the dirt all this time. Kinda makes a man worried." He nodded toward the high school. "Shall we?"

"How do you know where to go?" I wondered out loud.

"I follow the memories," was his answer.

I stopped walking and crossed my arms. "What do you mean, you follow the memories? We have memories everywhere, including the local jail."

He looked uncomfortable as he glanced away and then over my head, refusing to make eye contact. "He said our first stop was the police station, and I'd know where to go next. The day we set off firecrackers was the day—"

"Stop." My eyes widened. "No, he wouldn't, right? He's not…" It was my turn to get nervous. I stuck my finger into my mouth and chewed off one nail, then another.

Jason smirked. "Come on, where's your sense of adventure?"

"I left it back at the police station with the firecrackers," I said in a deadpan voice. "We're twenty-seven. We can't just…" I gulped.

"Exactly." He squeezed my hand briefly. "We're twenty-seven. We can do whatever the hell we want."

I shouldn't have squeezed back.

I did anyway.
My hand itched with need to touch his palm again.
I knew in my soul…
It was going to change me, that one touch.
I also knew I wasn't ready for a change of that magnitude.

chapter eighteen

"I've never truly been dumped, but the one close call happened when I told a girl that I wasn't sure I was feeling it — or her. She tried to beat me to the breakup, but I put on the charm and we stayed together one more day before I told her it was a test-run to see if we should keep going. I've never been slapped so hard in my entire life, but I learned a lesson that day. When it's time to go — you let it go. Closure is necessary in every aspect of your life, and if you don't get it, eventually you're going to get slapped, whether it be from the universe, or the other party."

~From Max Emory's Guide to Dating and Other Important Life Lessons

Colt

"Stop taking up all the room!" I elbowed Max hard in the ribs and watched in fascination as Jason held out his hand. "Take it! Take the hand. It's just a hand, nothing intimidating about a hand, don't just drop it after you touch it." Why the hell was I nervous? Like it was me? Maybe because I'd watched my best friend get his heart completely throttled by the one who got away. Or maybe because I wanted him to find his forever like I had. Ugh. I'd been watching way too much *Bachelor* with my wife, that was for damn sure.

Max snorted. "Speak for yourself. Mine are massive, poked myself, and others, in the eye several times. Not to mention, hands are a direct measurement of penis size. All you have to do is make a fist."

I dropped the binoculars and glanced over at both Reid and Max. Reid was busy shaking his head in dismay as Max made a legit fist and then frowned. "Wait, that's not right. It seems… oddly shaped."

"Your heart," I said through clenched teeth. "Your fist is the size of your heart."

Max placed his fist against his chest and shook his head. "Yeah, I disagree."

"Why, God? Why?" Reid muttered. "Max, you mean the thumb to the pinky finger. That's the size of a limp dick."

Max had to measure, again.

I missed my wife.

Home-cooked meals.

Damn spa weekend.

Damn Max.

She was relaxing, and I was on a stakeout with a guy who thought his penis was shaped like a fist!

In reality, I knew Max was a certifiable genius, but sometimes… I wanted to strangle him with my bare hands and make the world a better place. Hell, they'd probably throw a parade.

"Figured it out," he finally announced after much measuring, which had traumatized not only me, but the poor squirrels trying to eat close by. "'Tis your wrist to your elbow, fully erect. That's it." He nodded triumphantly and then winked.

"Never—" I rasped, "—and I do mean NEVER — wink at me again, especially after announcing how big your erection is."

"Jealous?"

"Got the girl, and you had to go on a TV show to find yours so… no, nope, not really."

"Bastard," he grumbled. "And I had twenty-five of those crazies after me. Plus, I got a goat out of the deal. Not too shabby."

"And a wife," I reminded him.

"Oh right, Becca." He grinned. And then laughed. "I'm kidding. Trust me, I know what I got in her…" his face fell. "Being alone sucks balls."

"Imagine being stuck with a psychopath," I offered.

He scowled. "Reid's different, but he's not a psycho."

"Thanks, man." Reid sighed and took a sip of coffee. "So, why are we sitting here watching them shoot each other *screw-me* looks while they contemplate holding hands in the parking lot?"

"Today was first-kiss day," I announced. "They hid back at the school under the bleachers, he made his move, she kissed him back, and so dear friends, their friendship went from playful to—"

"Sexual," Max interrupted thoughtfully, his fingers tapping against his chin as if he were thinking.

God save us from Max Emory thinking.

"I see where he went astray," Max continued.

My eyebrows shot up. "They're in the parking lot, walking toward the bleachers. There's literally no way he went astray then, or now. You can't go astray by walking."

"Listen close, young grasshopper." Max pointed to both of their retreating bodies as they made their way toward the field. "There's at least a foot of space between their bodies, her hands are limp at her sides, and she keeps clutching her fists. Our man is popping his knuckles, and they keep stealing glances at each other. If this is how he made his first move, no wonder things went south." He shrugged. "Jason lacks the pivotal movement that allows the woman to feel comfortable, confident, and sexy, all at once." Another pause. "He's not touching her back, he's not leading her, and he's letting her flail all on her own like a damn fish out of water. And fish out of water… they eventually die."

It was quiet.

Too quiet.

I stared at him in disbelief. Reid mimicked a similar look, as Max exchanged glances between both of us. "What? I know things."

"I'll be damned," I let out a breath. "I can't believe I'm about to say this—"

"Please don't," Reid interjected. "He's already impossible to live with."

"You're right." It was out before I could stop it.

Max grinned. "I have all the sex all the time, 'cause I'm right."

"And there it is." Reid rolled his eyes.

"A woman needs to feel secure, not vulnerable, not after what she's been through. Think of it this way…" Max licked his lips and narrowed his eyes, "if it started wrong, it can't end right."

"STOP MAKING SENSE!" I roared.

All three of us ducked when Jason and Maddy glanced behind them.

Max smacked me on the back of the head. We waited a few seconds, and then all looked again. They were back to walking, and I was back to wondering if the Jason I remembered ever had any game at all if he was twenty-seven and still struggling with the girl he'd always loved.

I tried to think back to my obsession with my wife, Milo.

And how I'd exhausted every resource in my arsenal just to find a reason to touch her, including dunking her in the pool; so yeah, near-drowning my crush was an actual move I had used during high school, but at least I'd touched her.

And Jason?

He'd been so close. He'd done the squeeze, and now?

He was touching air.

I frowned for the next few minutes and then sniffed the air. "Is that popcorn?"

Crunch, Crunch, Crunch. Max shoved a fistful into his mouth and offered me some.

And for the first time, I wasn't annoyed with Max — not at all — because underneath all of…whatever it was he had… he was right.

Maybe this was exactly what Jason needed.

chapter nineteen

"One of my many rules of dating is this: It's not about you. I know, I know, it feels like it's about you, but if you enter a date purely focused on yourself? You're going to miss the person sipping wine across from you. You're allowed five minutes to think about every insecure thing in your arsenal, the rest of the time is focused on making the other person comfortable. I guarantee that once they see what you're doing — they'll mimic it. That's what humans do, morons."

~From Max Emory's Guide to Dating and Other Important Life Lessons

Jason

My palms were sweaty.

I knew exactly what had been next.

So did she.

The first kiss.

The beginning of the end, when I'd crossed a line without asking, and she'd thankfully responded the same way. We'd been best friends up until that point. So many stolen glances between us, when we didn't think anyone had been looking. Nobody had called us out on it, but we were getting closer, and it was getting harder not to react to the way she made me feel every time she was close. As it was, I knew that if I touched her, I'd forget all the reasons I was angry and just kiss her, drink her in, and lie to myself — tell myself that she wanted me, when really, this wasn't about rekindling anything.

It was about ending it.

"Sort of feels like the end of an era, doesn't it?" Maddy smiled up at me shyly. "Like when *Friends* ended."

I grinned. "Wow, that's a heavy comparison."

She just shrugged and tugged her ball cap down so her eyes were a mere shadow. I hated when I couldn't see people's eyes. Maybe it was the cop in me, but I could tell a lot through eye contact, whether the person was open to giving it, or not.

And she wasn't.

So closed off.

Both of us.

I felt the distance spread until I was sick with it.

"Um..." she shoved her hands in her pockets, "...I forget how this started."

"Bullshit." I called her bluff, then took a step toward her and flicked her hat back so I could see her deep blue eyes. What I saw reflected in their depths gave me pause.

Fear.

Well, that made two of us.

I just wasn't sure what she had to be afraid of, when she was the one who'd left; she was the one who'd betrayed me.

So, there we stood.

The air thick with her fear.

My anger.

And the smell of fresh-cut grass, as the sprinklers flicked on a few feet away from us. The shadow of the bleachers above hid us from the sun. We'd joked about how it cloaked us from the teachers when it was absolute shit; they'd seen everything. They just hadn't cared — well, that, and they hadn't been able to control us when we were together.

We'd been the unstoppable duo.

Until Maddy put a stop to it.

My partner in crime.

The love of my life.

I wanted to turn away. I wanted to run. I wanted to yell and say this was stupid, but the longer I stared at her, the more I realized I was never given the chance to say goodbye.

She hadn't let me.

And I wondered, if we had handled it differently...

Would she have been able to leave in the first place?

Her breath came out in an uneasy exhale as she stood there studying me back; her eyes widened as I leaned down, cradling her cheek with my right hand like I had done back then.

My lips touched hers.

Asked permission.

With tentative velvet strokes, our lips slid against one another, slowly, as if it was a test we both wanted to pass with flying colors.

Her body relaxed into mine.

And then she was reaching between us, fisting my shirt with one hand, while gripping my shoulder with the other.

She tasted the same.

But her kiss was different.

More mature.

There was nothing uneasy about the way she slid her tongue past my lips. I opened my mouth to her, deepening the kiss. I tried to rein it in because, after all, our first kiss had been controlled. We'd laughed after then kissed again.

Tame.

It was so high school.

Then again, we'd been only sixteen.

But this kiss?

It said more than words could.

She moaned into my mouth when I moved my hands down, cupped her ass, and pulled her roughly against me as I attacked her mouth in a new angle. Maddy opened up to me as if she'd been waiting for my touch her whole life.

She cast a spell on me with that one kiss. My teeth nipped at her bottom lip as my hands moved into her hair, my fingers digging into her scalp, as we made out under the bleachers. She grasped at the loophole of my jeans, jerking my hardness against her and rubbing her body up and down mine as if she was just waiting for me to take her against the grass.

I heard nothing.

Felt nothing

Just Maddy's touch.

The smooth caress of her tongue.

And then her hand as she slowly moved it from the belt loop up my hard stomach.

"Damn it." I pulled away. It almost killed me.

Her eyes were lazy, her lips swollen.

"I, uh..." I cleared my throat, "...don't think we fully captured the awkward first kiss moment..."

She licked her lips and then, as if she still tasted me there, gave me such a lust-filled gaze I almost reached for her again, almost asked her if I could strip her in the middle of the field and make a new memory.

"Yeah, um..." she shook her head as if she was in a fog, "...sorry?"

I smiled. "Yeah, me too. Really sorry..."

Her lips twitched. "Oh yeah? What are you sorry for?"

"Stopping," I admitted truthfully. "You?"

"Almost copping a feel."

Not what I'd expected. I hadn't imagined it possible to get more aroused, and then she'd gone and talked about touching me. My length pressed against my zipper as she stared me down. "I'm disappointed you didn't act on it."

"Me too." She shrugged. "Then again, that would be cheating."

Cheat, cheat, please cheat! "Yeah." *Damn it!* "You're right."

"So..." she clasped her hands in front of her and rocked on her heels, "...what was after the first kiss?"

"As if you don't remember." I laughed. "Little liar."

She got so red she looked sixteen again. "We don't have to do that part…"

Hell yeah, we do. Best idea Max ever had. Not that I wasn't still pissed, but if it meant what was next, then yeah, I was all in. "My house or yours?"

"Yours," she said quickly. "Plus, if we're staying with the original day…"

"Uh-huh."

I grabbed her hand without realizing what I was doing. She squeezed back as we walked to the police cruiser. I helped her in, shut the door, and saw movement out of the corner of my eye.

Max was slapping Colt on the back, while Colt coughed and Reid threw popcorn in their general direction.

"Seriously?" I crossed my arms. "How long have you guys been here?"

Max frowned. "Jason? Is that you? The sun's in my eyes. Are you here for the annual movie night on the lawn too?"

I sighed. "Nice try. That's next week."

"Damn it," he grumbled, then opened his mouth as if he was actually going to try again.

I shook my head; he closed his mouth.

"No more free shows." I pointed at him and then stared at my other friends. "You guys actually followed Max for once?"

"I drove," Colt admitted.

"But only because Max doesn't have a license anymore."

I rolled my eyes. "Do I want to know why?"

Max shoved his mouth full of popcorn and shrugged, while Reid answered for him. "It involved a nun, a bicycle, and the goat. Trust me, it's too graphic for small ears." He pointed to Colt, while I busted up laughing.

"Son of a bitch! For the last time, I do not have small ears!" Colt yelled, voice raspy as if he'd just choked on a popcorn kernel.

Well, at least that explains Max hitting him.

"Sure you don't," I said soothingly, while Colt gave me the finger. "All right, I'm just going to leave you to your own devices. Try not to end up in prison at the end of the night."

"Wouldn't be the first time," Max said, mouth full.

"Exactly." I saluted them and got into the cruiser. "Everything okay?"

"Oh, yeah!" Maddy finished a text and looked at me. Her smile felt forced. "It's just… Annabelle gets cranky at naptime sometimes."

"Why's that?"

Her face fell as she swallowed hard and whispered, "She's afraid if she falls asleep, when she wakes up, I'll be gone."

"I know the feeling," I admitted without thinking, then heard her sharp intake of breath.

Shit.

I was losing at this closure thing. Especially when I let my guard down, and my anger forgotten. When I did that, all I had left was my honesty.

And my truth wasn't pretty; it was ugly.

It was a life lived without her by my side.

chapter twenty

"The first kiss is important. So important that every dude in their right mind better be nervous. But as I said before, it's not about you. Slowly, go into the kiss, press your lips against theirs, then, let nature take its course. Let nature decide those next few seconds, and do yourself a favor — make sure you're touching your significant other somewhere. None of this weird, a-foot-of-space-between-you, bullshit. Nobody likes that, except middle school teachers who like to kill pubescent joy one sad slow dance at a time."

~From Max Emory's Guide to Dating and Other Important Life Lessons

Maddy

My gut clenched.

I'd broken him.

Broken us.

Because I had been afraid… of so many things.

I'd broken the very thing I'd been afraid of breaking. *Stupid, stupid girl.*

My throat felt tight as we pulled up to his parents' old house. We'd exchanged the cruiser for his old truck again, which just made the tension that much worse, because the smell was enough to send me into a haze full of memories spent in that back seat, spread out for him to see.

I slammed my door shut and walked slowly toward the house.

"It's open," he said behind me.

A few inches, and I could lean back into his arms. Would he wrap them around me? Or push me away? My shoulders slumped as I opened the door and took a step over the threshold.

I didn't recognize a thing. It still had the same shell as before, but the old hardwood floors had been replaced with a dark-looking slate, the walls painted a warm tan color, and the pictures all replaced with more modern pieces that brought life into the house that I hadn't even realized had been missing. "This looks incredible!"

"Thanks." Jason stepped around me and down the hall into the open kitchen.

I could tell he was still working on it; the floor was all pulled up, and the backsplash was missing. All of the appliances were a shiny new chrome. The granite was a bright white. I loved everything about it.

"It's my side project."

"It looks like more than a side project. Did you pick out the colors and everything?" I ran my fingertips along the cold granite while he pulled out two water bottles and tossed me one.

"Yeah." He shrugged as if it was no big deal. "I had an apartment with Colt before he went off and got married to my sister. And after that, my parents decided they wanted to travel, so I get free room and board for redoing the entire house and putting it on the market, and they get free labor."

My heart stuck in my throat, as my brain tried to process the idea of him not living next to my parents. "You're selling?"

He gave me a funny look that made me feel somewhat stupid. We were adults, not kids, but still. "They're selling, but yeah, why?"

It felt like the end.

Like the final nail in the coffin.

The day that the Caro family no longer lived beside me.

I almost sank to my knees. What was wrong with me?

I didn't want to admit it.

Admit the reasons for coming back, for holding out hope that maybe… just maybe… things would pick up with Jason and me.

I scratched my head. "Nothing, it's just, where will you live?"

Can I sound any more desperate?

His lips twitched as he ran a hand through his messy dark hair. "Why are you so concerned?"

"Potential homelessness would concern any decent human being," I fired back.

He choked out a laugh. "I just got another promotion. I was thinking of buying my own place, maybe getting a cat…"

My eyes narrowed into tiny slits. *What game is he playing here?* "You hate cats."

He stared me down so hard — the way only Jason Caro could — that even my skin felt aware of his eyes as it erupted in goose bumps. "People change."

The air was thick with tension. I tried to breathe, but it was suddenly difficult.

"Honey, I'm home!" Max's voice echoed down the hallway as he appeared in the kitchen with Colt and the ridiculously handsome stranger.

"Hi." The stranger held out his hand; his voice was smooth and held a hint of arrogance that made me question his intentions, and then I saw the wedding ring, and then realization dawned. "I'm Reid—"

"The Phantom!" I hadn't meant to yell it.

He'd played The Phantom in *The Phantom of the Opera* before it left Broadway and would be starring in the newest rom-com releasing this month!

"Careful, your high school's showing," Max whispered out of the side of his mouth, earning a glare from Jason.

"Weren't you just on the cover of *Entertainment Weekly*?" I ignored them and bounced up on my feet.

"Aw, you saw it?" He turned his movie-star grin toward me.

Max moved between us and shoved Reid. "Keep talking,

and his ego won't fit next to mine, and that just puts me in a bad mood."

Jason groaned behind me. I turned and was surprised as his hand shot out and pulled me to his side, as if I belonged there.

I tried to tamp down the butterflies.

Just like I tried not to overanalyze what it meant.

I failed on all accounts and almost turned in his arms and asked him if that meant I could sleep over like old times.

Stupid kiss was really hurting my self-control.

Stupid memories of everything surrounding us, reminding me of what we'd had, what I'd left behind. And the more I thought about it — really thought about it — the more I questioned my decision. *Had I based it off fear alone?*

"Stop using the eyes on her!" Jason barked, making me jump. "Plus, you're married!"

"He can't help it," Max answered for Reid. "When you're an Emory, it just… happens."

Jason punched Max in the arm and grinned. "Sorry, when you're a Caro, it just happens."

"That shit hurt!" Max rubbed the spot and then turned his handsome smile back to me. "So, are we doing this or what?"

Colt made a strangled noise as Jason's grip on my body tightened. "You aren't joining us."

"But it was a pool *party*," Max pointed out, "and we need to re-create the actual event so you can move on and marry other people, right? Isn't that what you want, Jason? To move on with your life?"

Jason's grip loosened its hold.

Tears burned my eyes.

Why am I putting myself through Hell?

Oh, right. To gain his forgiveness and then what? Continue pining for him while he marries another woman? Why not just step on a rusty nail?

"Besides, we all know the real reason you couldn't marry Jane."

I felt my body tighten with anger. Jane had been the popular girl at school. The one everyone wanted to be — gorgeous, rich, and thankfully, stupid and selfish as well. I hated her. And the minute I'd heard that Jane and Jason's wedding was off two years ago, I'd almost driven back into town and groveled at his feet.

Pathetic, I know.

"Oh?" Jason asked. "You mean, other than you guys sabotaging the entire thing?"

"Details." Max waved him off. "You didn't have a heart then. You were like the Tin Man, awkwardly singing in the forest." He nodded enthusiastically. "But look what we have here." Max pointed at me. "Maddy's returned, so now you can get your heart back, slam it in its place in your chest, and bone the first woman who winks at you! Happily. Ever. After."

Colt groaned. "I don't think that's how this works, Max."

"It does." He said it like he meant it. "Oh, and I hope you guys don't mind." A few honks sounded from outside. "I scrolled through the invite list for the reunion weekend and invited some people who looked fun."

"Where the hell did you even FIND the list?" Jason roared.

I winced as Max just gave him a blank expression and said, "Does Superman reveal all his secret powers all at once? I didn't think so…"

"Are there no depths to where you won't crawl?" Jason

mumbled under his breath.

Max arched a brow. "I don't understand your question."

The doorbell rang.

And Max was off, peeling his shirt from his body, revealing a ridiculous six-pack, and rubbing his hands together as he whispered, "Show time."

I turned around and gave Jason a pleading look. The last thing I wanted to do was be at a party at his house, like we used to have, and see all my old, successful friends with their husbands and kids and lives and... I must have looked panicked because Jason grabbed my arm and pulled me down the hall. He shut us into the master bedroom.

There it was. The same bed we'd fooled around on, just because it felt naughty to make out where his parents slept.

Sixteen-year-olds.

"Hey..." Jason cupped my face with his strong hands, "...look at me."

I gulped and focused on his hypnotic eyes.

"I'll get rid of them. I'm sure I can come up with something. You can hide out in here."

My eyes narrowed. "Hide out? Why would I...?"

He took a step back, his face guilty. "Look, I'm not saying you need to be ashamed of coming back home. I just know that—"

"What?" I interrupted. "What the hell do you know, Jason? About me? About my life? My shame?"

"Whoa, calm down—"

NOT the thing to say to a woman. Ever.

"I'm perfectly CALM!" I yelled. "And I'm fine, totally fine with a party. In fact, maybe that's exactly what I need after a long day!"

"Long day?" He stepped back. "Long day? Are you saying

you hated it?"

"A trip down memory lane where I got to remember all the awesome things I did with the one man I'll never have? Yeah, it was a freaking blast! Can't wait to see what tomorrow holds, and for the record, I'm fine."

"You said that."

"Yeah, well." I lifted my chin at him. "It's because it's true."

"I believe you." He smirked.

How dare he smirk!

I narrowed my eyes and jerked open the door then marched down the hall toward Milo's room, where I knew I could find a bikini.

Once I got to the end, I paused.

"Top dresser-drawer," he called.

"I KNOW!" I yelled back then slammed the door behind me. Like a teen.

Well, one thing's for sure. This whole blast from the past was doing wonders for my maturity level.

Fantastic.

chapter twenty-one

"In the dating world, sometimes it's necessary to fight dirty. Very dirty. Oh get your head out of the gutter! I don't mean that kind of dirty. I mean, sometimes you gotta do the shitty hard work in order to get the results you want, ie: you may need to crawl on your hands and knees through mud and nearly get electrocuted before you get your girl, but totally worth it in the end. Because, who do you think nurses you back to health? And then you can really get 'dirty.' Feel me?"

~From Max Emory's Guide to Dating and Other Important Life Lessons

Jason

I FLINCHED WHEN the door slammed and then tried to hide my smirk as I walked back to my room and put on a pair of trunks. Honestly, I'd seen her panic and just assumed it was because she'd come home and didn't want to see anyone yet. I had no idea she was so insecure about the move, which just made me more curious about the missing ten years.

A decade. And every single day spent without her.

Laughter, and the sound of people screaming in fun, pulled me back down the hall and outside to the back patio. Maddy was nowhere in sight.

Max however, was.

I sighed.

He was the epitome of the word *enabler*; the guy was passing out tequila shots with limes. *Where the hell did he find a half-gallon bottle of tequila?*

"Jason!" Max yelled when he saw me. "Grab the keg from the car?"

"Keg?" I repeated. "What the hell, Max?!"

"KEG!" People around me screamed in excitement.

It was like partying with strangers. I didn't really recognize many people. John, a buddy from the football team, was with his wife, but that was it. Everyone else was only vaguely familiar. I would probably need a yearbook to compare pictures and smiles. After Maddy left, I hadn't exactly stayed in contact with people I went to school with — too much of a reminder, too painful.

"Hey, slugger." Liza approached, tequila shot in hand. "Killer party."

"Yeah," I croaked and looked away. Liza was the last person I wanted to see; her brother — and my ex-friend — was part of the reason for my misery.

Her face fell. "It's been ten years."

"Oh, really? Haven't been counting. Wouldn't know. I got a keg to grab." I smiled politely and walked off, fisting my hands tightly in anger.

Party?

Sounded like the best idea I'd heard in a long time, so after I grabbed all the alcohol from the car, including the keg and four boxes of liquor, I helped Max set it up while he yelled, "SHOTS!"

I quickly gulped down two rounds of Jack and wiped my face, just as Maddy came out of the house.

I started choking.

Not because of the whiskey, but because my spit had gone down the wrong tube.

She looked… edible.

Like I could sweep the vase off the dinner table, spread her wide, and just eat my fill until I was lost to her.

Full breasts spilled over a small black bikini, leaving little to the imagination, the top barely covering nipple, for that matter. And the bottoms? Well, she kept adjusting them.

Let's just say ten years later, high school bathing suits look small…

In the best way possible.

Head held high, she walked right by me to Max, grabbed a shot, threw it back then sucked the lime he'd held out in front of her.

I growled.

Max winked at me. "Something wrong, man?"

I reached for the non-existent gun at my side, which, obviously, just made him grin harder, as he kept handing out alcohol to parents of toddlers.

Because that was the type of party it was.

Almost everyone was talking about their kids, retirement, stock portfolios, vacation time, and babies.

It was almost too depressing for words.

I had most of those things, but what I'd always wanted…

A family. Babies.

Maddy.

She shared a sideways glance with me.

I reached for her, but she pulled away and ran full speed toward the pool and did a giant cannonball.

People cheered.

While I watched as wet, cold water ran down her curvy body. My gaze was so transfixed on her erect nipples, I was surprised nobody pulled me aside about my current situation of arousal.

Cold water. Fast.

I chased after her, jumped in…

And felt the warm buzz of alcohol fill my veins as I popped up and saw Max follow, nuts first, jumping right on top of me.

I ducked, just in time, so I didn't get a face full of balls.

The guy only laughed once we both popped up.

I swam to Maddy and tugged her against me. "Stop running."

"I'm not." Her breath came out raspy. "I'm just… reliving old times. Isn't that what you wanted? So we could have closure?"

Why does it feel like she is turning the tables on me?

"Yeah," I said slowly, "but—"

Her kiss was swift.

Hard.

Fast, and oh, so very punishing.

I plundered her mouth with my tongue like an eager teenager and pinned her against the side of the pool.

Music filled the air from somewhere outside, pounding into my ears the way I wanted to pound into her.

I grinned against her lips as she wrapped her legs around my waist.

And then a shadow, in the shape of Reid, cast over the water and started pouring vodka on our heads from above.

Maddy tilted her head back and opened her mouth, while I leaned in and licked it off her chin.

People cheered.

"Guys!" someone yelled. "Keep it down. Someone's going to call the cops!"

"Cops?" Max laughed loudly. "I am the law, bitches!" The music blared. "Plus, we already got our cop here." He pointed while I took another shot.

The crowd went crazy.

And then Maddy squeezed her thighs.

Yeah, the cops were coming, all right.

"Party Like a Rockstar" came on, just as more classmates jumped in the pool.

Laughing, I kissed Maddy again as the haze of alcohol filled my line of vision.

She stared me down, her eyes needy, her body arching.

I grasped her waist and then brushed my thumb across her right breast. She sucked in a breath, just like I'd expected her to do, as I pushed her body against the wall harder, my length pressed against her, straining for any sort of release it could get.

With wicked intent in her eyes, she reached below the water while music pounded around us.

Laughter.

Splashing.

And yet, it felt silent in our corner as she tilted her head and said, "Remember senior year?"

I gulped. "How could I forget?"

"Uh-huh."

Maddy slid her hand into my pants and gripped me so hard I saw stars, and when she moved, I braced my hands on either side of her body, resting my head against the curve of her neck, as I bit into her skin and tried to remember why I wasn't acting my age.

Shit.

Ten years.

Three women.

And this one?

This one had the touch I'd always been trying to replace.

Her fingers gripped around me and pumped harder.

I glanced around the pool in a haze as she jerked me in her hand as if there weren't at least sixty people partying around us, as if we were alone.

I was seeing stars when she suddenly stopped, right before I was ready to finish. I let out a growl and captured her mouth.

Her grip tightened.

I cursed into her mouth and pressed her so hard against the wall it was a miracle my dick hadn't pinned her there permanently.

"Are we really doing this?" I gave my head a shake. "Maddy…"

"I love the way you say my name." She moved her hand up and down.

"Want to be inside you," I said without thinking, then opened my eyes, ready to apologize, ready to say something like, *"Sorry, that was inappropriate,"* when she was literally jerking me in the pool.

She bit down on her lower lip.

"SHOTS!" Max called again. "Shallow end of the pool! Make a line!"

"They're making a line." She released her hand briefly, and then she was back on me again, guiding me to her core, to the side of her suit.

I shuddered at first contact.

"You gotta be fast."

"We're drunk. Buzzed, at least," I said as I moved against her. "People can see." Even as I came up with every reason we shouldn't, I already was.

"Live dangerously, Jason."

It was what I'd always said to her when I was daring her to do something, something which almost always ended up with us in detention. Warm water seemed to boil between our bodies as I pulled her farther into the deep end, toward the alcove of rocks where we'd often made out when my parents were home, and we didn't want to get caught. They'd shielded us just enough to keep us out of view.

I clung to her hand then pressed another kiss to her open mouth when the shadow of the rocks fell over us. *This… I need this, want this.* Her wet skin was so slick. I wanted to feel her around me, let the memory burn, let the pleasure bring more pain.

"Shit," I murmured when I realized my mistake. "We don't have a—"

"On the pill." She winked.

"Thank God." I surged forward, the water waving out from between us, and then I was pulled into her, sinking deep. And she let me. Her sharp gasp had me rock hard and needing more, wanting to create a freaking tsunami with each thrust.

Maddy wasn't just home to me.

This feeling, this thing between us…

It had been my forever.

Our eternity.

I knew I wouldn't last long.

Not with her.

Not like this.

Uninhibited, with the woman I'd never let go of, the one who was moaning in my arms and trying to bite down on my neck with each slow thrust.

We were already creating enough waves as it was, and I knew it was only a matter of time before someone asked where we were, or noticed the fact that there was unexplained violent splashing coming from the alcove.

"Harder." She bit my neck again. "Faster."

"Maddy—" I was losing control so fast it was embarrassing, "—any harder or faster, and they'll think a hurricane's coming. Besides, I want to last forever."

"Maybe later you can…"

It was all I needed as I surged forward, pinning her once again, filling her to the hilt as she let out a gasp and orgasmed around me with tiny bursts of release. And with each one, my grip on her hips tightened as my body violently vowed never to let her go.

I would say that it was easy.

But everything about me was still hard as I pumped two more times before falling silent in the deep end of my parents' pool, slightly drunk, surrounded by a party full of people I didn't remember.

Not one of my finer moments.

Not that I really cared.

Her eyes were glazed as she stared me down, as if all she needed was one more round — one more round I was more than willing to give.

"Jason! Maddy! Where are you?" Max yelled. "Your turn."

Maddy shot me a shy grin. "We already went."

I choked a bit before I slapped her ass, replaced her bikini that had been thrust to the side, and swam from under the alcove. I motioned for Max. "One more shot. Only one more."

"Sure, cop, sure…" Max said.

It was the last thing I remembered.

A likely story where Max was involved…

chapter twenty-two

"I'm not saying to get your friends drunk so they screw. All I'm saying is — well if you have no other option, why not try Jack Daniels? Seems to work on The Bachelor at least ten percent of the time, and when you're already losing, ten percent looks pretty nice doesn't it?"

~From Max Emory's Guide to Dating and Other Important Life Lessons

Maddy

My head pounded as if someone was building a house in my brain. I winced as I touched my temples and then opened my eyes.

People were spread out everywhere, lying on the grass, snoring, puking. Good times.

Well, we went out to relive high school. This looks like senior year all over again. I would laugh, but I feel like puking.

A bottle of water appeared in my line of vision, and then Jason was kneeling in front of me with a small container whose label indicated it was for said hangover.

Wait. I'd been so angry. And then there'd been shots.

More shots.

The pool…

My eyes lowered to the jeans he was wearing and what he was hiding behind that zipper.

I felt my face heat as I suddenly recalled all the naughty things we'd done in the water, in public, mere feet from everyone we'd graduated with.

"Tell me nobody saw," I whispered hoarsely.

"They were too drunk. Besides, we were under the rock alcove," Jason said softly. "Now, drink everything."

My stomach heaved as I chugged half of the water down, grabbed the pills from the tiny bottle that claimed to heal all hangovers, and chased them with more water.

"Give it ten minutes." He peeled off his shirt and handed it to me.

I looked down and groaned. "Did I pass out in this tiny bikini?"

He licked his lips. "Yeah. Trust me, it was torture."

"So, you're covering me for your sake?"

"That…" he put the shirt over my head, "…and if I see one more married man check you out, I'm grabbing my gun."

"Oh." My cheeks warmed. That was sweet, in its own way.

"You're beautiful, Maddy," he whispered, pressing a kiss to my forehead. I leaned into the warmth of his lips, closed my eyes, and just breathed him in, right about the same time I heard a horn go off.

It was loud.

Like something you'd hear at a basketball game.

Three gorgeous women — including Jason's sister — stood, arms crossed, surveying the damage.

It was obvious what they saw — barely dressed twenty-seven-year-olds lying around in disarray, beer cans, liquor, straws floating in the pool, not to mention the naked classmate still grasping the floating unicorn and sobbing about his divorce.

"MAX!" The one with dark hair stepped forward. "WHAT IN THE HELL!?"

Max stumbled forward and then gave his head a shake, as if he was trying to sober up but lacked the ability to follow through without the physical cue. "Becca? You're…" he swayed so hard to the right, I was afraid he was going to slam his head against the side of the pool house, "…here! Now we can celebrate!"

"Of course I'm here!" Becca smacked him on the arm. "You drunk-dialed me three hours ago and said you were drowning!"

"In alcohol," he mumbled. "But now, perfectly fine." He shrugged then tried leaning against the pool house, missed it by a solid foot, and collided with a lawn chair and a pink flamingo. He quickly got to his feet, clutching the neon bird to his chest, with a guilty look on his face.

Reid emerged from the house, weaving back and forth, and then used a person for support as he eyed the crowd. He sobered quickly as a gorgeous, curvy woman stepped forward. "I expected this of Max, not you."

Reid gulped and then pointed a finger in Max's direction. "Jordan?" he sputtered and then yelled, "He made me!"

The woman sighed and looked back at Milo.

"Tequisha." A slurred voice sounded as Colt rounded the corner with a bottle of Jack in hand.

"Colt?" Milo gasped.

"To be fair, I think he means tequila. I know nothing of this Tequisha bitch." Max nodded encouragingly and then narrowed his eyes at Colt and did an *"I'm watching you"* sort of thing with his hands that basically made him look even more drunk.

Colt dropped the bottle onto the grass and then hid behind Milo and whispered, "He's the devil."

"Okay!" Milo clapped her hands and shouted loudly. "Party's over! Please call an Uber. If you need to sleep it off, feel free to keep using the lawn, and using the lawn does not mean you are allowed to hump the garden gnomes." She cleared her throat. "Yes, you in the blue shirt? Keep doing that, and I'm shoving the gnome up your ass. See how good it feels then!"

"You feel me!" Max shouted as if he was somehow in on it.

Milo shot him a glare and warned, "Not now, Max. Not now."

"Not now, Max," he repeated in a soprano-pitched voice then held up his hand for a high-five from Colton.

"Slap his hand and never get laid again," Milo said when Colt had his hand mid-air.

He jerked it back and shook his head, while Max sent an evil look to Milo.

People moaned around us. Only about a dozen pulled out their phones and sloppily typed in their apps to get a ride.

I found my feet, thanks to Jason, and was starting to walk over to the girls when a pizza truck pulled up.

And suddenly, everyone was on their feet and running toward it as if it was a reunion concert for Pearl Jam.

Max crossed his arms. "Works every time."

"Evil genius," Reid scoffed then slowly stumbled toward the truck. He grabbed two boxes and motioned toward the house.

Jason pressed his hand on my back, guiding me toward the patio door, as Reid dodged inside just ahead of us and placed the boxes on the kitchen table.

Things were a little blurry after that.

We all sat down.

Max tossed paper plates.

And then it was just all of us moaning while the sober ones gave us looks of pure judgment.

Cheese draped down my chin. I sucked it in, wiped my face with a nearby napkin, and pointed at Max. "He called everyone."

"Bought the booze," Colt added.

"Forced tequila." Reid looked ready to puke as his wife tried to force him to take another bite in an effort to sober him up.

"His fault," Jason agreed, sounding the least drunk of us all, which had me wondering just how sober he'd been a few hours before when we'd been in the pool.

I felt my body tingle just thinking about it.

His hand moved to my thigh.

And the tingles just kept coming.

"I'm very disappointed in you." Becca pointed her cheese-laden pizza at Max. "I mean, what kind of father are you going to be if you just lead everyone astray?"

Reid choked on his swallow, while Colt stared straight at Becca and said clear as day, "Take it back!"

"Take what back?" Becca grabbed her water with one hand then placed her other hand on her flat stomach. "Are you still drunk?"

Reid gasped.

And Jason made a cross motion, muttering, "God save us — or *it*."

"You're pregnant?" Milo gasped, then pulled Becca into her arms.

"Yes!" Becca started to tear up while Jordan — who I assumed belonged to Reid, since the other two were taken — gave him a sly smile and winked.

Okay…

"You too?" I blurted out toward Jordan.

Max took a look at his brother, shrugged, and said, "Those Emory swimmers work fast."

Milo gagged.

Colt patted her on the back soothingly, as if he, too,

understood the visual depravity it gave.

"What?" Max shrugged. "It's true. I bet mine even beat Reid's. If there was a race between my sperm and his, his would just give up and die while mine would hit—" He slammed his hands together. "—home—" Another slam. "—every—" Slam. "—damn—" Slam. "—time."

Jason moved his hand from my thigh and covered my eyes. "I'm sorry you had to witness that."

Everyone burst out laughing while I tugged his hand down and smirked.

Max just shrugged and said, "Slam," again, earning a few tossed napkins in his direction and a full water bottle from Reid.

Nice.

"You're full of shit," Reid sneered. "But also, congrats. That's awesome, man."

"Thanks, bro." Max grinned. "You too."

"Aw, guys..." Becca wiped under her eyes, "...I love it when you get al—"

World peace between Max and Reid had lasted about five seconds, and then suddenly, the earlier thrown water bottle was chucked back toward Reid's head by Max.

He dodged it, and it went soaring...

Into Jason's face.

The plastic bottle slammed into his perfect nose and then sprayed all over the table.

"Son of a bitch!" he roared, as blood ran out of his nose. "Seriously, guys? Can we not have at least one normal meal where someone's not trying to kill me?"

Max reached across the table to grab him napkins but, no doubt because of his drunken state, instead knocked over my Diet Coke and created a brown trail of bubbly, all the way to Jason's crotch.

Jason didn't retaliate, or even make a noise, just sat there and stared daggers at the man responsible for it, as the entire thing emptied on the front of his shorts and blood trickled from his chin.

Becca jerked Max back while I grabbed the napkins and held them out to Jason, his eyes still on Max as he took them and patted his chin.

"You missed a little." Max pointed, but Becca slapped his hand down.

"Thanks," Jason said in a tense voice.

"Anytime, man. What are friends for?" Max said all casual-like, as if he wasn't the reason for global warming or, at least, for Jason's chaotic state.

"So…" Milo cleared her throat, "…you four need to go clean up the back yard."

"Four?" Max crossed his arms. "There were five of us."

I shook my head. "Traitor."

"That rock alcove looked mighty fun…" Max grinned while I let out a horrified gasp.

Before I knew it, a fork was flying toward Max's face. He ducked, just before it stuck into the wall behind him. "Jason Caro!" Max yelled. "You nearly beheaded me!"

"It slipped."

"MY ASS!" Max surged to his feet.

"Let's use all this energy for clean up," Becca said cheerfully, slapping Max on the ass and pointing him toward the back door. "Off you go, or I'm canceling naked time."

Max pouted. "But—"

"One, two—"

"I'M NOT A CHILD, BECCA!" Max roared, then stomped out of the house.

The rest of the guys begrudgingly followed.

"Huh," I wondered aloud. "Does that work on all men?"

"Oh, the countdown?" Milo answered for Becca. "Colt says it gives him anxiety in his balls."

"Reid likes it when I'm dominant like that." Jordan just sighed into her bottled water.

"You never know though," Becca piped up. "Jason might be all over that. I used it once on Max. One time, and he did the dishes for a week naked because he was afraid of what happened after three."

We all fell into a fit of laughter as the back door opened and Max poked his head around the corner. "I HEARD THAT!"

"THREE!" Becca yelled.

Complete silence.

chapter twenty-three

"When a woman starts counting, you only have one choice, you get naked, and you do whatever she says — nobody wants to know what's after three. Nobody."

~From Max Emory's Guide to Dating and Other Important Life Lessons

Jason

"So—" Max cleared his throat awkwardly, "—never knew you could do it in a pool, and so fast. Inquiring minds would like to know."

Reid and Colt both stopped picking up trash and looked up, smug expressions on their faces, as Max leaned against his rake.

"Was it your lack of… skill? Or was the water just really putting up a fight for your initial, uh, entry."

"Max." My teeth clenched. "Listen very carefully. I am the law. I will end you and make it look like an accident with planted evidence and enough cocaine to make you New Haven's biggest pimp. Don't, just… don't."

"I've never done cocaine." Max seemed thoughtful. "I think it would be bad for my heart."

"You're like the lovechild of Barney from *How I Met your Mother* and Schmidt from *New Girl* — but with a severe cocaine addiction and no warning bell."

"Ha!" He laughed. "No, but seriously… drugs are bad."

I groaned.

"Man has a point," Colt spoke up. "How long did you disappear for? One, maybe two minutes?"

"Bullshit!" I roared. "It was at least seven!"

"Seven, seven, seven." Max started humping the rake. "Oh, sorry. I was thinking of the *Friends* episode where

Monica draws the graph — funny, since I have my own graph. Maybe you should look at it. Might change your life."

"I don't need a damn graph!"

"Quick!" Max dropped the rake and crossed his arms. "What's a two, three, six?"

I stared — I mean, *really* stared — wondering if I was about to be witness to one of Max's brain cells exploding out of his ear. "What the hell are you talking about?"

Reid raised his hand.

"No!" I jabbed a finger at him. "I call bullshit on Max."

Colt cleared his throat, then looked guiltily away, while Max just grinned and said, "Or how about a triple-seven?"

Reid actually groaned.

"You don't have a graph." I shook my head. "And even if you did, I'm not looking at it!"

"Changed. Colt's. Life." Max winked.

"YOU SWORE!" Colt picked up the rake from the ground and pointed it at Max's lifted hands. "ON THE BIBLE!"

"First off, I had my fingers crossed behind my back. Second, I lied. It wasn't my Grandma's Bible. It was an old copy of *The Hobbit,* still sacred, still doesn't count."

Reid snorted out a laugh.

"Like *you* never looked at it," Max taunted.

Reid shifted on his feet and coughed. "Maybe once or twice."

"He has it memorized," Colt offered.

I looked at the three of them.

Is this what marriage does to men? Makes them gossip about graphs and sexual positions over beer instead of watching football like a normal person?

"It's laminated," Max added in a cheerful voice.

"Waterproof."

I wiped my face with my hands and said in a gruff voice, "I'm an incredible sexual partner."

"Two minutes—" Reid coughed.

"It's been a while!" I fired back. "All right?"

It slipped.

My confession.

I had their attention.

"I think I want to see the graph now," I muttered.

"No, let's stay in this safe circle of trust," Max said soothingly. "How long, exactly? Are we talking days… months…"

I looked away.

"…years?"

"Year," I snapped. "I've been busy, thanks to you."

"Ah yes, my signs." Max nodded slowly. "But really, can't you at least squeeze in a few one-night stands? A year? That's… Well, Jason, I hate to say it, but you're like the male version of being pregnant. It's just no fun — no alcohol, no soft cheeses, no comfort in bed. Look at you! You're past nine months and can't even see your ankles! Shit, man! Pull yourself together."

"You lost me at pregnant," Colt added.

"Same," Reid and I said in unison.

Max sighed. "Come on, it's graph time."

"What about the mess?" I looked around the littered lawn.

"Even prisoners get bathroom breaks," Max muttered.

"Been to prison much?" I laughed.

"We've been over this. No more empty threats, Jason, especially when I'm about to change your life."

Colt rubbed his hands together while Reid jogged after

us.

The house was quiet except for the low hum of the TV.

Huh, maybe the girls went out?

We rounded the corner and walked down the hall and into my dad's old office. All of his things were still in their place. It was the one room I hadn't touched, because I didn't have the heart to mess with the crown molding. His large mahogany desk filled half the room, and his leather chair made a squeaking noise when Max dropped into it and then felt underneath the desk as if he was searching for a key.

"The graph's here?" I tapped the glass top.

Max looked slightly guilty as he felt around and then pulled out an honest-to-God laminated graph with a woman drawn on it, numbers on her body, complete with a color-coded key to the right, typed out like a freaking worksheet. "Your dad found Colt's copy then got curious. What? I'm a giver. I let him have the original, and he hid it from your fox of a mom and told her he'd just been working out more and reading her *Cosmo* at night."

"Stop." I squeezed my eyes shut. "Just stop."

"What?" he laughed. "They're old, not dead. Am I right? Plus, that mom of yours has sexy legs—"

"Max!"

"Fine." He slid the graph cross the table. "Welcome to the Promised Land, my friend. Eat, eat, eat." He stopped chanting and then pointed to the numbers. "May I suggest starting slowly? Maybe with a one, seven, one, so you're stimulating both her breasts and her—"

"This is what hell must be like," I interrupted.

"Don't be a prude, Jason. Real men ask for help. That's what we are, real men!"

Real men looking at a graph on how to please a woman. A

graph made by Max. Friggin' genius.

God, I hate him sometimes.

A knock sounded at the door, and then it cracked open.

And like a room full of middle schoolers caught with a Playboy, all of us fumbled around until I finally just sat on the desk on top of the graph and exhaled.

The door opened.

"What's— What's… up?" I drummed my fingers against the glass covering the desk.

"Wow! Two what's?" Milo's eyes narrowed. "Why are you guys in Dad's office?"

"Strategizing," Max said in a clear voice. "Why else would we be in here? I mean…" he started to nervous laugh, "…it's not like we're looking at porn!"

"That would be weird," Reid added with another burst of laughter.

"Max…" she crossed her arms, "…why's Jason sweating?"

"How the hell do I know? Maybe he has an STD from chlorine?"

"Huh?" Milo squinted.

"Max, stop talking," I said in a hushed voice. "Anyway, we should probably get back to work."

"Yup!" Reid agreed, too quickly, while Colt stretched his arms and yawned, walking past Milo as if he hadn't gotten advice on how to please her from another guy.

While my sister watched them leave, I slid the paper out from behind me with my fingers.

Max jerked it and hid it on his person.

Milo stopped us at the door. She cleared her throat then held out her hand.

Max hung his head then slowly pulled the sheet out from under his shirt and handed it to her.

"Good boy." She patted him on the head. "And you missed eight."

"THE HELL I DID!" he roared.

She just winked and said, "It was a later addition. You can thank Colt for that one."

"Son of a bitch one-upped me?" He stomped away, yelling Colt's name and shouting something about pistols at dawn.

"How you holding up?" Milo asked, her eyes serious.

I sighed. "I'm good."

"You look stressed."

"I'm always stressed."

"She's back," Milo said softly.

I gulped and braced myself against the doorway. "Yeah, caught that."

"Just…" she squeezed my arm, "…if you need me, or need to talk… I'm here."

"I know." I bent down and kissed her forehead. "Love ya, sis."

"Hey, Jason…" she reached out and grasped my hand, "please… be careful, all right?"

Too late.

"Sure," I lied, and walked away feeling as if time was already against me.

chapter twenty-four

"The Graph will be available in PDF form on the Max Emory website, as well as available in the back of the book. Might I suggest printing two copies just in case? And trust me, you really do want to get that bad boy laminated. Hell, I know a few that have it framed; it's sacred, anything sacred deserves your tender loving care, just like your penis."

~From Max Emory's Guide to Dating and Other Important Life Lessons

Maddy

I WASN'T SURE how Milo would treat me. I mean, the last time I saw her, I'd been getting ready to run away from her brother.

From a family who had always felt like my own.

I'd expected her to ask me why, not offer a glass of wine while we all sat outside and watched the guys work.

Becca cupped a hand around her mouth and yelled, "Take your shirts off!"

Max scowled. "I'm not an animal, Becca."

"You literally asked me to call you tiger last week when—"

"BECCA!" Max actually blushed and then, with jerky movements, pulled his shirt over his head. "There. Happy?"

I sucked in a breath; the man had an impressive pair of abs, which was all sorts of confusing, since he seemed like the type of guy who was allergic to exercise.

I was probably gaping because Becca looked over at me and just shook her head in obvious disbelief. "I gain weight from Diet Coke, and that one literally spent a week eating nothing but Krispy Kreme and actually gained an extra ab."

"Bastard," I huffed.

"And he sits. He sits all day long. Yeah, he goes for runs, but he's not running for the sake of running. He's running to practice for the *zombie apocalypse*, his words, not mine."

Milo choked out a laugh. "You should have seen him in

college. He used to tree-dodge in case they'd learned how to hide on the branches."

Becca just sighed out, "Gotta love him."

Colt peeled his shirt off next.

Milo whistled while he did a little *Magic Mike* dance her direction.

A pain sliced down my chest. I wanted that. I wanted… a relationship. I wanted… something.

And all I had was my stupid heart reminding me that I'd had it.

And let it go.

Jason didn't take off his shirt.

And it felt uncomfortable saying something in front of Milo; she was being kind to me, but I knew if the situations were reversed, I'd be pulling her hair out and shoving her into the pool.

I was protective of my family.

My friends.

Not that she wasn't.

Maybe she was just more mature.

"Reid, Jason!" Jordan called. "Don't be the only losers clothed. Take it off!" She tapped on *The Weekend.*

Jason flipped us all off for at least five seconds, earning boos, and then finally relented and pulled off his shirt. Reid followed suit.

"I think my heart just stopped." Jordan fanned herself. "Those men are lethal. It's almost unfair."

"I agree," Milo piped up. "But Jason… I mean, I get that everyone was in love with him and Colt in high school, blah, blah, blah, but he looks so much better now, like he finally filled out, became a man. Right, Maddy?"

I choked on my spit, pounded my chest, and finally bit

out an airy, "Yeah."

Milo grinned. "He got addicted to lifting weights the way people get addicted to pie. It's kind of stupid how much muscle he has."

"I'm sure he's lethal," Becca added, "you know, on the force and other places…"

I felt my cheeks heat as I chugged more wine. *Is it unreasonably hot out here?*

Milo started fanning my face.

I hung my head. "That obvious?"

"Girl…" Jordan refilled my glass, "…they can see your lust from space."

We fell into fits of laughter as the guys finished cleaning up.

"Yeah…" I shrugged, "…I can't help it. Look at him."

Jason's skin was bronzed from the sun. There wasn't one muscle that he hadn't completely beaten into submission and grown. Hell, I wasn't even sure I could find an inch of fat on that man's body — but I'd love the opportunity to do a little research.

Visions of his mouth on mine, his hands in my hair, assaulted my brain until I was drooling over him like a loser with my mouth open.

His tongue had been hot.

His hands firm as he'd gripped my hips, as if he'd known just how to handle me and had wanted to throw me around a bit.

I sighed.

"Can I ask you something?" Milo said quietly.

"Sure." I was sure I knew what was coming. I sucked in a breath, braced myself, and waited.

"Why did you run?"

The girls were silent, each of them staring at me, waiting for the whole sordid tale, when there really wasn't one, just like there wasn't a great reason other than my own insecurities about our future.

I hated myself more in that moment than I ever had.

Because my future had been in front of me.

My love.

And I'd turned on it and hadn't allowed myself to look back for ten years.

Jason deserved better than what I had to offer. I'd known it then. I knew it now.

"Sometimes, we do stupid things, make decisions for other people based on what we think will happen. Jason loved me without a plan. I left him because I needed one in order to feel secure, and the last thing I wanted was for us to be eighteen-year-olds without a college education, a home, a future. I didn't want to end up like my mom." There, I'd said it. I didn't tell them about the whispers I'd heard from other students about being a local girl and ending up just like my mom. I was too ashamed.

And I was already feeling like the worst daughter by mentioning my mom.

She'd done everything for me.

Never anything for herself.

Had kids, didn't go to school, never worked a day in her life outside the home, and my biggest fear had been turning out just like her.

And resenting him, and our love, because of it.

"And now that you're back?" She hadn't probed further about my mom, but something told me she knew it wasn't her place. This was between me and Jason… and the chasm of hurt that filled each year I'd ignored where I'd left my heart.

In his hands.

"I'm back to take care of Annabelle here." I swallowed the ache in my throat. "My sister isn't in the picture anymore, and it was getting too hard to do it on my own, so we moved back in with Mom and Dad. I was an editor for a while, but it didn't pay enough, and with Annabelle in school and me trying to be the mom more often than not, it just wasn't in the plan." I'd left out the part about my sister randomly leaving for days on end, or my favorite… leaving her little girl alone in the hallway of my apartment building to wait for me to get home. Terror filled me just thinking about it.

"That's it!" Max yelled. "We're done being your slaves. Feed us, or suffer the consequences!"

And just like that, the moment was broken.

And I was so thankful I could have cried.

I glanced over at my house.

Mom was outside with Annabelle, watering the plants. I'd been gone most of the day; it was about time I went home.

I slowly got to my feet and went back into the house, careful to clean the wine goblet before grabbing my purse and making my way toward the door.

"Leaving without saying goodbye?"

Jason's deep voice caused every hair on my body to stand on end in a magnetic, please-keep-talking way.

I looked over my shoulder and smiled.

Why does he have to be so good-looking? So commanding that the room stands at attention waiting for his next few words?

"I've been gone for a while, and Annabelle gets grumpy if she doesn't see me."

"When's her bedtime?" He moved closer.

I frowned. "What?"

"Answer the question."

He was crowding me, making it impossible not to smell his cologne, and the mint gum on his breath, and feel the heat from his body. "Um…" I felt dizzy in his presence. "…eight. I read her a story at eight, and she goes to sleep. Why?"

"Eight-thirty, it is." He leaned down and kissed my cheek.

"But…" I frowned, "…if I remember correctly, after our first kiss and our skinny-dipping episode, which we didn't really—" My voice faltered. "We're still doing that? Didn't the whole…" I gulped, "…you know…"

"No, you should spell it out, sweat a bit more, and keep looking at the button on my jeans like it's going to fly off at any minute." He grinned.

I pressed a hand to my hot face. "I meant—"

"Eight-thirty." He bent near and kissed my neck. "Don't be late."

"Wouldn't dream of it." I breathed a sigh of relief when he walked away, only to be crushed with mounting anxiety as I walked back to my house and noticed that the chalk line he'd always kept drawn on the cement was almost gone.

I tried not to let it upset me.

But it was impossible.

He had been my world.

And now, we were living worlds apart.

chapter twenty-five

"Be the bigger man, even if it means you look like a complete tool. I've been the bigger man all my life. Now look at me... total tool, but alas, I got the girl."

~From Max Emory's Guide to Dating and Other Important Life Lessons

Jason

It was a warm summer night. Everyone was in the house cooking, drinking wine, and hanging out.

My foot still throbbed, but other than that, I wasn't really feeling any pain.

Maybe it was because of Maddy.

Maybe it was the pool.

Or maybe it was just that all of my friends were back in one place, Max not included.

Or maybe…

I eyed her bedroom window.

How many times had I crawled up the side of the house and stolen a kiss? Or just held her while we slept in her bedroom?

Her light was on.

I imagined her lying on her back, on her favorite white down comforter, and staring up at the fake stars I'd put on her ceiling.

One for every twinkle I'd seen in her eyes.

Meaning, I'd stuck three hundred stars up above her.

And made her swear never to take them down. Were they still there? Staring down at her? Protecting her when I couldn't?

My gut clenched. I had no idea what I was doing. The anger was still simmering, but every time I tried to grasp it, it was almost as if it had turned from something liquid to steam, rising through my fingers until I was left with nothing.

My pride had stung when she'd left.

My heart had broken in pieces when she'd chosen him.

Levi Tice hadn't been back in town for years, but I still remembered the day he'd gotten in trouble with the law. I had not only arrested him for public drunkenness, but had jabbed a few good hits in — pure self-defense.

"The great Jason Caro!" he slurred. "Hey, weren't you supposed to go to some big school? Play ball? Did the lure of donuts hold you back? Or were you just waiting for Maddy? She ain't coming, man. Trust me. That girl was meant for bigger things than a washed-up quarterback."

Each word had been like a punch to the gut.

I'd actually chosen to do online courses and go to the police academy because it had been an actual passion — and because passions changed. I'd loved football, but I'd known I could never make a career out of it, and my body was already seeing the effects of seven different concussions. So, I'd made a choice.

From the outside, maybe it had appeared that I was waiting for her.

Maybe, I'd never stopped.

I checked the clock on the wall. Eight-thirty on the dot.

With a deep breath, I moved through the house and opened the front door. The sticky summer heat smelled like barbecues and beer. Gravel crunched beneath my feet as I slowly limped toward her house.

Maddy was already there, waiting.

And she was on her knees, drawing a pink chalk line across the cement like we used to do.

"Nice color choice." I crossed my arms.

She grinned up at me. "Real men wear pink."

"Real men shouldn't," I smirked.

She just laughed and dropped the piece of chalk back onto the ground then rubbed her hands together. "So, what's the plan?"

"It's eight-thirty," I whispered then took a step toward her.

She'd changed into a pair of black leggings, Nikes, and a black hoodie. She looked athletic, cute, still beautiful. I inhaled her scent and then took another step closer, until we were toe to toe. "What happened every night at eight-thirty?"

Maddy's eyes seemed to drink me in. I wanted to dive my hands into her strawberry-blond curls and pull them close to see if they still smelled like coconut lime verbena.

"A kiss goodnight." She finally got the more than two words out, her eyes filling with unshed tears as she looked between the chalk line and my lips.

I had no idea what the hell we were doing now, where the line began, where it ended. I didn't know if she would walk away after this, or if we really would get closure, and lay our demons to rest.

But I needed it — I needed her.

We were both sober.

She could say no.

I could yell and tell her I hated her for breaking my heart.

The world could also end, and Max could be voted president.

But in that moment, nothing mattered but her kiss, her

mouth on mine. The moment her lips pressed against my lips, I prayed for time to stop so I could hold on to the second that things felt right again.

My heart soared in my chest.

This wasn't giving me closure.

This was making me want something dangerous.

It was making me want Maddy.

chapter twenty-six

"Life is easier when you finally come to the conclusion that it's probably your fault — whatever it is — and there's only one way to fix it. Take a long, hard look in the mirror, and start making better choices so you're not immediately ashamed of your own damn reflection."

~From Max Emory's Guide to Dating and Other Important Life Lessons

Maddy

My heart hurt.

His lips were smooth, which just reminded me of how sharp the pain had been when I'd sat in that car and drove with Levi into the city.

I sent a quick text to my mom to let her know that I was okay.

It was a lie.

I didn't count the tears; there were too many.

And Levi's constant optimism didn't help either. I'd chosen him because I'd trusted him, because I knew he wouldn't ask questions or hit on me.

There was no way to explain an actual broken heart to a person. Words for that feeling don't exist in the human language.

The worst part of leaving Jason was that I expected him to jump into his truck and tear after us.

He didn't.

He stood still, unlike time.

And faded into my past, just like his figure faded from the rearview mirror.

I never heard from him again.

Suddenly angry, I jerked away from him, shoving against his chest.

He stumbled back a bit on his hurt foot and winced. "What the hell was that?"

Now I was really pissed. "You never chased me!"

"What?" He threw his hands up in the air. "Are you serious right now?"

"You— you just— stood there! You were in track. You could have chased me, could have forced me to come back. You could have driven into the city and burned down my apartment to get my attention. You just..." salty tears hit my lips, "...stood there."

Jason hung his head. "I was in shock, Maddy. I had proposed to you twenty-four hours before you hopped into a car with Levi. No explanation. You just left!" His chest heaved as he clenched his hands into fists.

"Because I was afraid! But that doesn't mean I'd wanted to! That doesn't mean things wouldn't have been different if you hadn't just choked!"

"Choked!" he roared. "What damn part of this aren't you getting, Maddy? You left me! With one of my best friends! What the hell did you think was going to happen? That I'd force you to come back? How many hits do you think my pride needs? My mom had already sent the engagement news to the local paper. It ran the next day, while I sat alone in my room staring at the fucking ring I'd saved for years to buy for you!"

More tears spilled in rapid succession down my cheeks as he yelled, as he forced me into his pain.

"I wouldn't leave my room." Jason looked away; his voice had a hitch to it as if he was either choking up, or trying not to. "I just stared at pictures of us and wondered if it had all been a lie —if you even cared — because you don't throw away forever in an instant."

My heart slowed as he lifted his hands and put them behind his head then kicked the pink chalk with his good foot.

"You broke my heart, Maddy. I've never hated, and loved, someone so much in my entire existence."

"I was afraid." My voice was small, unsure.

"Of us?" he asked.

"Of hating you like you hate me now… of coming home one day and forgetting why I was so lucky to have you by my side… of resenting staying home at eighteen, not going to NYU, not experiencing — anything. I was afraid of our future. And then the whispers about us being another local couple that bites the dust. That same night, Liza overheard someone asking if I was pregnant; it was just too much. All of it was too much, too soon. And I thought, 'Is this just some fantasy we'd both conjured up,' and then when you didn't chase me…"

"So, you threw it away," he answered, in the silence as the sun set around us, blanketing everything in dusk.

"My mom…" I tucked my hair behind my ear, "… she's… as happy as she's capable of being, but she's… I've always been…" I frowned when Jason came closer and held out his hand. I took it and continued, "…afraid, I guess, that I would end up just like her — no education, no career. Funny, since I ended up just like her anyway, only worse, because I'm living in my old bedroom."

Jason tilted my chin with his right hand. "Maddy, futures don't just happen. You choose them, and those choices are like rocks that line your path. You planned that path perfectly, but left me off it by assuming I wanted to settle, when all I ever saw as I looked at you — was my greatest adventure."

My body jerked to attention as my mouth dropped open

then closed. "I—" Tears burned my eyes. "—I'm so sorry, Jason…"

His lips were on my face.

Kissing one cheek.

Kissing the other.

Caressing my forehead with his mouth as he whispered against my skin, "It's been a long day. Why don't you go lie down?"

I nodded, not trusting myself to say anything more.

Not trusting my body not to fall into old habits and just cling to him for support and strength.

Not trusting my heart to stay where it belonged, but instead, jump out of my chest and beg to be held.

The air around me was silent as I slowly walked back to the house and wondered what reason I'd ever had for being upset that he hadn't chased me.

When he'd just made it painfully clear…

It had never once occurred to him that he would ever have to.

chapter twenty-seven

"When the world seems against you, it probably is, so put on your big-boy pants, take a shot, and make the world your bitch, but only after recognizing it's always been your oyster."

~From Max Emory's Guide to Dating and Other Important Life Lessons

Jason

I STARED AT her house a few more seconds before turning around to the sound of clapping.

Max was leaning against the door. He picked up his wine glass from the ground along with the bottle and lifted them to me. "Might I suggest some vino after that little… outburst?"

I snorted and took the bottle. "You heard?"

Max whistled. "Your grandma heard, and she's in a home, hours outside of the city, with a pair of noise-canceling headphones and an addiction to *Riverdale*."

"Noise-canceling headphones?" I just had to ask.

"Oh, I never forget Christmas, and she's such a good receiver — just ask Reid." He winked while I literally felt my balls tingle with fear. A few years ago, the woman had attacked Reid with nothing short of super-human strength and a tube of ChapStick. She was basically the poster grandma for good-touch-gone-bad.

The guy still had nightmares — just another thing Max liked to discuss in his book and also, film for his blog.

"I didn't chase her," I admitted out loud, "but I was in shock, and by the time the shock wore off, I was so pissed, so angry, so sad—"

Max pulled me in for a hug. "Get it out, big guy."

I shoved him away, causing wine to slosh out of the

goblet. "I'm not hugging it out. I'm still pissed. I'm confused. I'm—"

"Horny." Max nodded. "Because you've tasted, and now you're addicted."

He wasn't wrong.

"But probably a bad idea to do that again until you have all this shit cleared up between you guys. Sex rarely makes things easier."

I just stared at him in shock. "I hate it when you make sense."

"Read my book!" He threw one hand up in the air. "Seriously, I'm your best friend—"

"Colt's my best friend."

"—so you should have already read it, memorized it, and left a five-star review on Amazon. Seriously, that's how you feed authors. You give them stars."

"Stars," I repeated, my mind wandering to Maddy, lying in her room, looking up at the stars. My curiosity was killing me to find out if they were still there.

"Staaaaars…" Max dragged out the word. "You know, the things in the sky…" he pointed up, then sighed, "…at least, during the night."

"Yeah." If she'd kept the stars, did that mean she still felt something? Hell, I was acting like I was a teen again. *Circle yes or no!*

"Look…" Max wrapped his free arm around me, "…it sounds like she freaked out, bolted, and that you, in all your anger and — let's admit it — pride, decided to just move on to the next psychotic bitch who gave you bedroom eyes."

"Jane?"

"SHHH!" Max shoved me away. "Do you want her to appear?"

I frowned. "She lives in the city now."

"Doesn't matter." Max trembled. "Never matters." He grabbed the wine glass and threw its contents over his shoulder. "Let's just hope this vino works like salt, since it contains alcohol."

"None of what you just said makes sense," I pointed out.

"I can't be brilliant all the time. Even God got a day."

And back to making sense again.

"You guys have one more day to get your closure," Max explained, "but might I suggest another option?"

"You'll share, even if I say no."

"Only a best friend would know me that well."

He smiled while I cursed myself for having spoken.

"You could always kiss and make up, ride off into the sunset, or... grab the ring I know you probably kept in the left side of your underwear drawer, and propose."

"Back up. How the hell did you know that?"

"Best friends." He grinned and then grabbed the bottle of wine from my hands. "And I got bored and snooped. Didn't take you for a man-thong sorta guy, but if that's what gets your gun all snappy, who am I to judge?"

I groaned. "It was a gag gift!"

"The tag was off."

"There never was a tag!"

"Dude, calm down. I don't judge. You should see what's in Reid's drawer. Actually, it's under his bed. The spreader bar didn't fit in the drawer."

"Thanks, man." Reid appeared in the doorway and gave his head a shake. "So cool of you to hack into my Amazon account and send me screenshots of all my own purchases while on set."

Max shrugged. "Not my fault the director was looking

over your shoulder when I sent the shot of the Zip Ties and Fifty Shades Your Way, Mr. Grey."

"It was for Jordan."

"Good sexual appetites are never reason for judgment." Max held up his hands innocently. "At any rate, this isn't about Reid's weird 2:00 a.m. Amazon purchases of sex toys, or even about my ability to hack his account every time he changes his password. It's about Jason either getting closure, or getting his girl."

Colt poked his head outside. "You bitches gossiping?"

"I am APPALLED!" Max pointed at him. "I've never been anyone's bitch—"

"Max!" Becca yelled, and honest-to-God, the man jumped into the air and ran into the house so fast he almost tripped over the rug.

"Sometimes I think we just keep him around for the constant entertainment," Colt said to himself and then gave me the look — the look best friends give other best friends when they have free advice to offer. "Jason…" he rubbed his lips together, "…I think— Wow, I'm going to need to ask you to run me over with your truck later, but I think Max has a point." Air whooshed out as he slapped his chest with his hand. "Why was that so damn hard to say?"

"The universe doesn't like it when we take his side." Reid shuddered as a swift summer wind picked up.

None of us moved.

It stopped immediately and we all sighed in relief.

"My point exactly," Reid muttered. "And as much as I hate myself for agreeing… why not see what's there? I mean, the reunion's tomorrow night. You guys still clearly have chemistry…"

The wind picked up again. And I had the sudden urge to

duck and cover to avoid more lightning.

"Go, young grasshopper!" Max was back in the doorway with Becca behind him. "Find your truth!"

Becca groaned, while Colt and Reid just shrugged and nodded toward her bedroom window.

"And try to be romantic." Max snorted. "None of this almost-getting-hit-by-a-car-or-lightning-strike shit. Also…" he pointed to the house, "…real men climb."

"Climb?" I repeated.

The guys all grinned.

"Find yourself some rocks, then search around for your balls, since you've clearly lost them," Max smiled wide, "and shimmy up that damn house and tell her how much you've missed her, and then, when she's primed, naked and—"

Becca clapped a hand over his mouth and winked at me.

With a sigh, I waved to everyone and limped across the chalk line and onto their property.

It was a little after nine, now. The lights were dim in her room as I knelt, grabbed a few rocks, and tossed them up at her window.

The curtains pulled apart.

And then the window was raised, and she poked her head out. "Jason?"

"Can I come up?"

"You aren't a teenager anymore, Jason. What if you fall and break a hip?" she teased, leaning over the windowsill with nothing on but a white racerback tank and a wide smile that had my body tightening in all the wrong places, if I was going to attempt climbing to her second-story window. Her white teeth sucked in her bottom lip as tendrils of strawberry-blond kissed her shoulders.

Like hell was I going to stay on the grass a second longer.

"You've got this!" Reid.

"I believe in you!" Max.

I muttered a curse and started scaling the tree outside her window like I used to in high school. I was stronger now, so pulling myself up to the first branch was cake; though somewhere in my heavy, lust-filled brain I realized that I'd been struck by lightning, so maybe climbing a tree and stumbling across an old roof hadn't been the smartest choice I could have made, but she was smiling at me, and I could see in her bedroom window, and it just felt — right.

I stepped away from the tree and onto the roof.

Easy street.

I sent her a wink as I took another step.

And then made it all the way to her window without falling through the roof or tumbling off it.

"The universe agrees!" Max yelled.

"What's this about the universe?" Maddy asked, holding out her hand as I ducked into her bedroom.

"Ignore him. He used to buy holy water in bulk, just in case my ex came back to haunt him."

"Seriously?"

I nodded. "Yeah, but I think he just wanted an excuse to put in a bulk order from the Vatican."

She laughed.

"I'm serious!" I did a slow circle.

The posters were gone from the walls, and the pink had been covered over with a mute tan that made the room look more grown up. Everything was different.

A jolt of disappointment hit me as I tried to keep my smile in place when uneasiness pulsed through me.

Nothing was the same.

What the hell had I been thinking?

That I would crawl through that window like old times and step into my senior year with Maddy?

I sighed and sat down on her bed then said the only thing I could say that made sense, "I missed climbing into your window."

"I missed watching you climb." She sat down on the bed next to me and put her hand on my thigh. "But I think I missed you more."

"You think?"

She grinned. "Maybe a tiny, small bit more."

With a sigh, I lay back and put my hands behind my head then let out a little gasp as the hundreds of stars twinkled down at me in all their cheap glory, right along with a picture of Maddy and me at prom.

She cleared her throat. "I didn't… I couldn't…"

I gripped her hand tightly. "You kept them."

"They're a part of me," she whispered.

I squeezed my eyes shut.

"Jason?"

"Yeah." I kept them closed, afraid if I opened them, I'd see her, see how beautiful she was, and do something insane like try to seduce her in her old bedroom with her parents sleeping across the hall.

"I know ten years is a long time. I know that you can't possibly forgive me for what I did… But do you think maybe you can try? So we can be friends again?"

My eyes snapped open, locking on hers as I whispered, "No."

Her face fell.

"Yes to the forgiveness, yes to moving on, yes to everything, but, Maddy, I can't — nor will I ever be able to — be just your friend."

She swallowed slowly as her eyes darted between my mouth and my eyes.

I leaned up on my elbow then reached for her with my free hand. I tugged her close, until our foreheads touched. "Forgive me for not chasing you with every ounce of strength I had, for not screaming your name until you came back. Forgive me for letting my anger and hurt cripple me into less of a man. Forgive me?"

Tears welled in her eyes as she nodded her head yes. Her breath fanned against my face; she smelled like coconut. Her skin felt hot and smooth. I cupped her cheek and closed my eyes. "I'm going to kiss you now, and then I'm going to go so I don't do something I can't take back."

"You already did something you can't take back," she pointed out. "Or at least *we* did. What's one more time?"

I groaned. "I've never had self-control when it comes to you, Maddy, and now that we're adults and we make our own choices, my self-control is even less because I don't give a shit if your parents walk in on me licking between the valley of your breasts while squeezing one of your nipples between my fingers, just to hear your sharp intake of breath. I really don't. But I would hate a repeat of last time…"

She shoved me and laughed. "When my dad chased you with a shotgun?"

"I almost died that day!" I said, earning a pillow to the face. "Do you know how freaked out I was? I literally hid in the tree house for five hours while he searched for my body with a gun, flashlight, and one of his hunting dogs — all of this because I was making out with you in the basement!"

"Hey now." She laughed harder. "You had your hands up my shirt."

"They were cold."

"Sticking with the same story, huh?"

"It's ironclad. He couldn't prove they weren't cold, and he couldn't prove your body was warm." I shrugged. "Damn, I was even a good cop back then."

She tilted her head, a wide smile forming across her lips. "You were a lot of good things, Jason. Still are."

I leaned in and brushed a kiss across her soft lips then stood, trying like hell not to show her how hard I was for her, how much I wanted to slam that bed against the wall, pin her body against the mattress, and forget about the world.

"Maddy?" Her dad called her name.

I felt actual fear of her father even at twenty-seven.

With another quick peck, I was out the window and walking back to the tree. I was almost to the first branch when I heard his voice get louder, as if he was ready to look out through the curtains, and when he finally did, I was under the cover of multiple branches.

"I heard voices," he said in that same voice that, to this day, gave me chills, and I loved the guy. He ate breakfast at the diner every morning with his paper and cup of coffee and, most days, even bought me my own breakfast.

But when it came to his daughter?

I was still eighteen.

And he still had a gun.

Then again, so did I.

"Hello?" he called out the window.

"Daddy," Maddy said in an annoyed voice, "I was on the phone with Liza. Seriously, go back to bed."

"Hmmm." He pulled the window down with a jerk.

I exhaled and waited a few minutes, trying to guess what she felt, where this was really going, then turned on my heel.

And walked right into a body.

I knew that smell.

I knew that body.

I looked into his steely-blue gaze and cleared my throat. "Nice night."

"You climbing into my daughter's room like a coward, Officer Caro?"

"No, sir." I wasn't a coward. "But I was climbing into her room like a man. You got a problem with that?"

He stared me down.

I stared right back.

And the wild, wild West suddenly came into that yard, each of us reaching for our non-existent sidearm, as a tumbleweed rolled past. Hell, I could even hear Max singing the theme from Tombstone.

"All right then." He stepped back and scratched his bald head. "But the roof's a bit old — patched it up last year. Next time, use the door like a human."

"Yes, sir." I smiled as he walked off.

He paused and called over his shoulder, "Still got that shotgun, Officer. Law says if your dead body's on my property, it's self-defense."

"That it does."

"Nice night, though. Real nice night."

The screen door hit him on the ass on the way back into the house, and I exhaled as if I'd just been through war and come out unscathed.

I had a smile on my face the entire way to the house and until I made my way upstairs and saw a naked Max just sauntering down the hall as if it was normal.

"CLOTHES!" I roared.

He stopped, looked down then up, and shrugged. "I'm not going to put on clothes because I intimidate you. So hey, how'd it go?" He started biting on a carrot.

"Becca!" I yelled.

The door to one of the guestrooms opened. She poked her head out and sighed. "Stop sleepwalking and get to bed."

"He's sleepwalking, and he has conversations like this?" I asked, confused.

"He does his best work at night, trust me. The guy writes out crazy plans on his laptop, goes to sleep, and then he wakes up, remembers absolutely nothing. How do you think that last health-care bill was concocted? This guy had sex, fell asleep, got hungry, went to the kitchen, slipped, and thought, '*You know what would be great?*' Weeks later, it was passed in Congress."

Max just kept chomping down on his carrot.

"I think it's God's way of protecting humanity, making sure Max's genius only exists when the world is sleeping, and he has no recollection of his own awesomeness."

"Huh, good point. All right then, I returned the stray. Have a good night." I reached for the bedroom door about the same time Max shouted,

"Self-driving motorcycles! Eureka!"

chapter twenty-eight

"It's easy to get caught up in the moment — hard to actually stop, process, and decide if that moment is going to change you forever, or ruin you for life. Enter Jason Caro. Tweets encouraged and welcome!"

~From Max Emory's Guide to Dating and Other Important Life Lessons

Maddy

"THAT BOY, JASON, climbed into your daughter's window last night," Daddy announced over breakfast, earning a giggle from Annabelle and a worried glance from my mom.

My parents knew how hard it had been for me to leave, and Mom understood more than anyone how much I'd loved him, how much I still loved him.

The day I found out he was engaged to Jane, I called my mom, sobbing.

The day of their wedding, I had a bottle of wine and Netflix for companions, only to find out that the wedding was off.

Bittersweet was how that felt. I was sad that he was probably upset, but happy for myself. Even though I knew I'd messed up too much with Jason, I still felt like I had hope.

I shook myself from my memories. And after last night, I had more than just hope.

I had a real reason to think things could be different between us again.

I had the whole weekend off and a whole lot of time to think about what that meant for both of us.

I ignored my parents and helped Annabelle get dressed and ready for the day. A knock sounded on the door shortly after.

"Officer Caro," Daddy snorted. "Come on in. You want some coffee?"

Jason's green eyes latched onto mine with such intensity, it felt as if our lips were already touching as we breathed each other in.

"No, I was just coming to pick up Maddy."

He held out his hand.

A sense of déjà vu washed over me as I took it and left the house with a kiss to my dad and a wave to my mom and Annabelle.

"Your dad…" Jason shuddered as he walked me toward his house, "…still terrifying."

"He's harmless." I rolled my eyes.

Jason just stared me down. "The man's tried to shoot me twice, hardly harmless."

"Protective?" I offered.

"A little." Jason snorted. "All right, I think I have everything ready to go."

I frowned, "Everything?"

"Yeah…" He looked suddenly uncomfortable, "…and before you say anything, know that this is Max's idea. He thinks it's going to help us get over the whole you-leaving thing, me being pissed, and all of that." Jason chewed his lip, apparently nervous, as we walked into the house. "He said to just bring you here and get over it."

Food had been placed buffet-style in the kitchen, and everyone was gathered around the TV.

Max pressed play.

I sucked in a breath as Jason and I appeared on screen, he in his graduation gown, me, in mine.

People were walking around us, celebrating our

accomplishment of finishing twelve years of school. But not everyone.

No, Jason was busy getting down on one knee.

One by one, people quieted, until he had the attention of most the senior class. With a confident grin, he said the words I'll never forget.

"Maddy, I want to spend the rest of my life with you. I love you. You're it for me. Please, say yes. Say you'll be my forever. Marry me?"

My smile was forced.

My fingers shook as I let him put the ring on my left hand as I nodded and pulled him in for a kiss, because I didn't trust my mouth to form the word, "yes," when my heart was screaming. "no, not yet!"

People cheered.

And I started to cry.

People probably assumed they were tears of joy.

They'd been tears of fear, tears of dread.

Tears of absolute heartbreak.

And then the whispers started; the video picked them up. Whispers about getting knocked up, divorce bets, cheating bets, and laughter about the local girl never making anything of herself. "Knew she'd be stuck here the day she got into NYU."

The room was silent around us… extremely uncomfortable, but somehow necessary.

Jason gripped the edge of the table he was leaning on so hard his fingers turned white. "I never watched it."

"What?" I had to have heard him wrong. "You never watched the proposal?"

He shook his head. "Too painful… and now I really wish

I would have."

My chest ached as Max slowly rose from the couch, followed by everyone else. Noises of them grabbing food and talking in hushed tones suddenly filled the very small living room.

I needed to sit.

Jason didn't move.

I hugged a couch cushion to my chest and waited.

He exhaled slowly and then turned his glare to me. "You weren't even excited."

I opened my mouth to speak.

He just shook his head. "Those weren't tears of joy, Maddy. I mean, what the hell? Why even date me? Why stick with me so long? Make me think you loved me and then pull that shit?"

"Ja-son—" I choked on his name, my tongue suddenly heavy, "—you know why. I wasn't ready. We weren't ready. I was so afraid, so damn scared I'd resent you eventually, or you'd resent me. I just… I know you saw us as an adventure — you said so last night — but when I saw our path, it was so uncertain, I just panicked! Plus, didn't you hear them? All of the people whispering about us? I didn't want us to become a statistic. I was young, stupid!"

"You didn't trust us." He sighed. "You didn't trust me."

Tears spilled over my cheeks as I confessed, "I knew Levi was leaving the next day for the city. I was sure that he wouldn't say anything to anyone — especially you."

"Oh yeah, why's that?"

"Because he was jealous of you, all right? He always had been. You had everything he wanted. He was backup quarterback, never really had a girlfriend, and here you are, the golden boy. It was one thing he could take from you, so

I let him. And he did."

The room was silent.

Jason nodded then grabbed a pair of keys and slammed the front door behind him.

Tears welled in my eyes as Max, Colt, Reid, and their wives, all came back into the room.

Becca hit Max with a pillow, followed by popcorn, Twizzlers, and, from Colt, almonds.

"Stop!" Max grabbed one of the thrown pieces of licorice and shoved it in his mouth. "Well, that went worse than I thought it would, but he needs to get the hell over it. He's a grown-ass man. So, man up!"

"It's not that easy," I admitted.

"Love never is," Max fired back. "You think it was easy trying to land someone like this?" He pointed to Becca, and she beamed. "You think it's easy when I doubt myself every day why she hangs around my brand of crazy? And I mean, most days, the only reasons I have are my bank account, perfect body, face, and giant—"

"What Max is saying," Becca interrupted smoothly, "is that love tests us all. You have to decide what you want. Do you want closure? Do you want his forgiveness? Or do you want him back?"

"Option C" Max mouthed.

I smiled down at my hands. "I want him back."

They erupted into cheers.

Milo stared me down. "Hurt him again, and I'm telling your parents about the night you snuck out and had sex in the tree house."

I gasped.

Max nodded with a wink. "Get it, girl."

"Do it," I leaned back, "and I'll just tell Colt about the

time you saw him naked in the locker room and took a picture."

"Nice." Max held up his hand for a high-five.

Colt batted his hand away. "You had a naked picture of me?"

"It was for Human Anatomy class!" Milo said with red cheeks then narrowed her eyes at me. "Senior year, homecoming, when you and Jason snuck into the faculty room, and then the principal's office, stripped in front of his desk and—"

"Candy anyone?" I held out a bowl of M&Ms and nodded to her. "You have my word."

She grinned and dusted off her hands while Colt pulled her in for a kiss. "You're evil."

"I know." Milo sighed happily.

chapter twenty-nine

"Rejection is like being offered warm peas as a way to bring the swelling down after getting kicked in the balls. So, what do you do when you get handed said vegetable, and you feel your balls hiking back up into your body? You get pissed at the pain and, eventually, it goes away. Come on, there is no easy answer to pain except to fight through it and know one day, it's going to be gone."

~From Max Emory's Guide to Dating and Other Important Life Lessons

Jason

I GRABBED A six-pack of beer — not one of my finer moments since it was eleven in the morning — then trekked across the football field and sat in the end zone. I could almost feel the heat of the lights, the cheers from the crowd. I'd loved playing football.

I'd loved her more.

Everything I'd done had been for her. Had it mattered? Had I?

I was on my second bottle when Max's car pulled up. Reid, Colt, and the devil himself, piled out in silence then joined me on the grass. They passed around a flask, and then Max handed me a sub sandwich, as if that would make it all better. He was like the Italian who solved everything with food.

When I didn't grab it, he took it back, unwrapped it then held it to my closed lips. "Eat, eat," he urged.

"Soak up the alcohol, big guy." Colt slapped me on the back. "One bite, and then you can have this." He dangled the flask in front of me.

I took one large bite and washed it down with the worst tasting whiskey God ever created. "What the hell was that?"

"Max's creation." Reid shuddered. "I grew two hairs on my chest last time I drank this shit."

Max rolled his eyes. "He exaggerates. Hairless cat, that

one."

Reid flipped him off.

"It seems like just yesterday…." Colt leaned back on his elbows, apparently reminiscing. "When the hell did we get so old?" He pointed to the stands. "Maddy used to make the largest signs with glitter, scream her head off, and lose her voice over your stupid throws on the field, remember?"

How could I forget?

My eyes had searched for her every time I ran out.

I still blame the State loss on her getting the flu and not being able to make it. I'd been in such a weird funk that I'd thrown three interceptions and had been sacked five times. It had hurt like hell, until I saw her concerned face, and her lips had made me forget all about the pain. She'd been everything.

"Yeah," I croaked out, reaching for the flask again. The sweet burn was doing nothing for my current mood; if anything, it just made everything seem darker.

What the hell had I been thinking?

Being with Maddy again hadn't brought closure. It just made me question every moment we'd had together and wonder why it had been real for me, when it hadn't been for her.

"She loves you," Colt said in a quiet voice. "I know she does."

"That's the thing about love. I could have sworn it was being reciprocated all those years ago, and here it is again, begging me to believe in it, when all I want to do is shut down."

"Look at it this way," Max piped up, "if you don't forgive her, if you don't chase her this time, some bastard's going to scoop her up, and then where will you be? I'll tell you. Bitter, alone, and eventually dead, with a donut sticking out of your mouth. Your gravestone will say, '*Here lies Jason Caro, struck by lightning but ended by frosting.*' It's sad, man. So sad."

Reid punched him in the shoulder, but Max apparently wasn't fazed; he kept staring me down with that intense look he got when he was being serious, and for some reason, if this was causing Max to be serious, it forced me to want to believe him, to listen.

"Your call," Max said. "But if I were you, I'd sweep right into that reunion barbecue tonight, kiss her on the lips, and then take her into the tree house." He waggled his brows. "How many times did you do the deed in there anyway?"

"How do you even know about the tree house?" I wondered aloud.

"Milo threatened Maddy with it, then Maddy threatened her back. It was like a really hot chick-fight with no punches thrown, just words," Max's eyes glazed over. "But words… sometimes those are so much hotter."

I handed him the flask.

"Ask yourself what you want, Jason," Reid joined in. "Do you want her? It's a simple answer. Stop thinking about all that other bullshit and answer, yes or no."

"Yes," I whispered.

"Will you fight for her?" Max asked next.

"Yes." I hung my head.

"All right." Colt rubbed his hands together. "We have four hours until the barbecue starts, and right now, Jason smells like beer and whatever the hell Max puts in his whiskey. Let's get him fed, cleaned up, and ready to rescue the girl from her tower."

I didn't say anything.

I just thought the words.

Felt them in my soul.

She was the one saving me.

Always the one saving me.

My light.

My soul.

I'd always felt like she was better than I deserved, and when she'd proven me right, a part of me had died inside.

I wasn't sure I could handle it again.

chapter thirty

"You gotta fight, for your right... to partayyy.' Truer words never spoken — shout out to The Beastie Boys for understanding life, and shout out to my buddy, Jason, for taking it by the horns and making tiny little party babies with it. You know what you did, and I'm proud of you. Also, you were wrong. I looked awesome in prison, and I learned how to knit! I'm coming for you, Martha!"

~From Max Emory's Guide to Dating and Other Important Life Lessons

Maddy

COLT TEXTED MILO.

Jason was coming, which meant I actually had to go to the reunion. It was going to be held out on the quad of our old high school. The theme was Friends Forever, and it kind of made me want to puke in my mouth. Then again, that had been our slogan throughout senior year. Everyone had been so happy… we'd loved each other… *Yay, friendship bracelets.*

Our class had literally earned the most detentions in the school's history. It had been so bad, our senior prank had been to litter the principal's door with them. We had so many combined that we had been able to create a trail out of the office and down the hall.

Over eight hundred and seventy-two pieces of pink paper.

It had been a beautiful sight.

Until our principal's eye had started twitching, which Jason, of course, had pointed out, earning him yet another detention — with me, since I'd laughed with him.

We hadn't been the best kids.

But we'd sure had fun.

I wouldn't change any of it, except for how it had ended.

Funny how people often want to change the middle of the story, the boring part, or the part that builds into this beautiful crescendo.

But me? I always hated The End.

And The End I hated the most, made me look in the mirror and realize that the reason I felt empty, was because I was afraid.

"You ready?" Milo asked once we were out of the car and walking toward the large group of old classmates.

"No," I admitted. "The other day everyone was too drunk to even ask me a question. They'd just wanted to party. Plus, I was with Jason the whole time. This almost feels like I'm about to be naked in front of everyone."

"While Jason would probably prefer that…" Milo laughed, "…it's not going to be so bad. Trust me. Ten years… well, people change a lot in ten years. Add in kids, jobs, stress, family, and we're all just trying to survive the best way we know how."

I linked my arm in hers. "Thanks."

My tall heels clicked against the pavement as we got closer, and my legs started to sweat beneath my skinny jeans. I'd decided to go for a simple white strappy tank, only dressing it up with my heels and a few layered silver necklaces.

Milo, however, looked dressed-to-kill in a sleek, multi-colored maxi-dress and hoop earrings. She'd always been the wild one out of all of us. It made sense that she and Colt would be a great fit.

I rubbed my sweaty palms on my jeans as Liza ran up to me and pulled me in for a hug. "Word on the street is that you and Jason are hooking up."

I rolled my eyes. "Stop listening to the elderly gossip."

"But Blanche finally stopped threatening everyone during happy hour. Get this, she doesn't even make the busboys cry anymore! Plus, she has all the dirt on your man."

My man.

I gulped.

My man.

Let's hope so.

I tugged down my shirt and gave her a weak smile. "We're just talking right now."

"Good to know," a familiar deep voice said from behind me.

I completely froze, as a cold sweat broke out.

Horrible timing.

The worst.

I pasted on a smile and turned. "Hey, Levi. Good to see you."

"Weak!" He stared down at my outstretched hand. "Only a handshake for the guy who bailed you out of this place?" He pulled me in for a hug before I could stop him, and that was about the same time Jason walked up looking hot-as-sin in a pair of fitted jeans, a tight black shirt, and a pair of Ray-Bans that made him look like a rock star.

"The hell!" he roared, lunging forward then jerking Levi away from me.

I was so thankful I could have cried. Levi and I didn't talk anymore, and to be honest, he'd only made me feel awkward after that day, as if somehow, I'd helped him screw over one of his best friends. It was a gross feeling, one I'd tried to forget until now.

"Whoa!" Levi held up his hands and laughed. "What are you gonna do, Officer? Arrest me for hugging a sexy piece of ass?"

Liza gasped and mouthed, *"Sorry,"* to me.

She left out the part that her brother had turned out to be a giant jackass. From the bits and pieces she'd given me since I'd been back, I'd gathered that he'd been dropped from two Canadian football teams early on, before coming back home with his tail between his legs and working at one of the prestigious car lots that only dealt in foreign cars.

He had quit school.

Quit everything.

And was clearly bitter.

"I'd watch what I say," Jason growled, still fisting Levi's shirt between his fingers.

A few people started whispering and walked closer to us.

The very last thing I needed was a scene.

"Jason, let him go," I pleaded.

"Yeah, Jason, let me go, like she let you go," he sneered.

I covered my eyes, but peeked through, as Jason swung. His fist connected with Levi's jaw, and then his nose, and then a good stomach punch, before Reid and Colt pulled him off.

Levi lunged, just as Max stepped in front of him.

Max swore as he stumbled backward after earning a punch to the face, then cracked his knuckles and whispered, "Oh, this is gonna be fun. Haven't been in a brawl in so long. Come at me again, and I'm going to make you feel me in a way that nobody wants to be felt, got it?"

Levi just sneered and tried again.

Max not only blocked the punch, but snapped Levi's arms to the side and threw a kick to his stomach, sending him crashing against the cement.

The guy ran his mouth as if he was afraid one day he'd be given a limit on words. Who knew he could fight?

Levi stood up again just as Reid stepped forward and earned a, "Pretty boy," comment that had another punch being thrown. Reid somehow fell against a bystander, who shoved him, and with all the testosterone flowing, the skirmish had turned into a giant fistfight that was only stopped seconds later by sirens.

"Well, well," Jason said as one of his police friends — by the looks of his smirk — handcuffed Levi. "It's not detention when you're not in high school anymore."

And then I was arrested right along with Levi, Milo, and Becca — who had just arrived and seen Max throw a kick and had assumed we were getting attacked.

Our classmates stared at us in horror as we were shoved into cop cars, and I wasn't sure if I was relieved or pissed.

chapter thirty-one

"'Good things happen in prison,' said no one ever. Word to the wise, if you want to prove your manhood to your woman, just pull it out and show her, feel me?"

~From Max Emory's Guide to Dating and Other Important Life Lessons

Jason

"I KNEW WE would end up in jail," Milo groaned. "I had an inkling, and I ignored it. I should have listened."

Max adjusted his jaw. It cracked as a bit of blood dripped down his chin.

He didn't look as bad as I felt, as I begged Mendoza to let us out. I gripped the bars and bit back a curse. "Mendoza, this is bullshit. I was defending myself."

The officer on the other side of the bars sucked on a lollipop and grinned. "Oh yeah?" He pulled out a folder. "Looks to me like you threw the first punch after you got offended by that tool over there."

"That's abuse!" Levi shouted in a separate cell next to ours. "I want my attorney."

"Oh, you do?" Mendoza said in a serious voice. "You hear that, Jason? He wants his lawyer."

I rolled my eyes. I knew what Mendoza was doing; the guy was king at talking shit.

"Let me think about it." He tapped the lollipop against his teeth then shoved it back in. "Nope."

Levi slammed his hands against the cell. "This is bullshit. I did nothing wrong!"

"You kidnapped a woman when you were eighteen, but sure…" Max said from his corner, obviously peaking Mendoza's interest as he looked between the two.

He jerked his chin up. "That true, Levi?"

"She came willingly," he said in a bored voice. "And that was almost ten years ago! She practically begged me to save her from this guy! Clearly, he's insane. Look what he did to my nose!"

"Stitches." Mendoza shrugged.

Maddy hugged her knees to her chest and glared at Levi.

"I practically rescued her," he sneered.

"That's it!" Maddy shouted then dropped her feet to the ground and made her way over to the bars separating our cells. "I asked you for a favor because I knew you wouldn't try anything. I thought you wouldn't ask questions. But instead, the first thing you did when you got me into the city was ask if I would thank you properly with 'a ride for a ride'!"

I saw red.

Absolute red.

Mendoza gaped. "That true, dipshit?"

Levi looked at me and then away. "It was forever ago. Kids say stupid things."

"I had just ruined my life, and you wanted sex!" Maddy screamed. "How dare you betray my trust like that! I lost everything! Everything!"

She was shaking the bars so hard I was afraid she was going to take down the jail cell.

I moved toward her just as Mendoza buzzed the door open, grabbed her by the arm, and pulled her out. "Go home."

I wondered if he remembered the trauma. He was three years older than us, but it had been the talk of the town.

How Jason Caro had lost the love of his life.

I hung my head as the cell door closed. Sure, I could have escaped, but what would be the point? Maybe I needed to suffer some more. I'd had no idea that bastard had put his hands on her. If I'd known, I would have actually killed him, rather than just physically altering the shape of his nose.

Maddy didn't look behind her.

Didn't say goodbye.

Just walked out, and I was reminded of another time, when she'd been afraid and had done the same thing.

I wanted to fight.

I wanted to chase her.

I wanted so many things.

But in that moment, I wondered if there had been too much bad blood, and if we'd ever really be over that day.

Or if we'd continue to relive it as if it was happening all over again.

Six hours later, the rest of us were released.

Six hours later, a six-pack of beer, pizza, and I were sitting in my living room, staring at the wall, wondering where I'd gone wrong in defending her.

It wasn't until sleep had nearly overtaken me that I remembered the look of embarrassment and horror on her face when I'd punched Levi.

Bad call, Jason. Bad call.

chapter thirty-two

"Sometimes, when I need good life advice, I watch Toy Story. Stay with me here, folks. There is nothing that you can't defeat in life without the mantra, 'Never give up, never surrender.' I dare you to try to stay defeated with that little gem hanging around your head. You're welcome."

~From Max Emory's Guide to Dating and Other Important Life Lessons

Forty-Eight Hours post-jail

I TIPPED BACK the lukewarm Corona and glanced at the flickering TV. Alone. Again. I deserved it.

A knock sounded at the door.

I ignored it and reached for another slice of cold, hard pizza. How long it had been sitting in my living room, I hadn't a clue.

I'd lost track of a lot of things in the past week.

My truck door for one — my fault.

My heart — her fault.

My balls — the universe's fault, not to mention an unfortunate run-in with lightning.

And finally, my ability to move on.

It was easy, the first time you moved on from a lost love. Life happened. Days came and went. You chalked it up to the fact that you'd been immature and stupid. Hell, you were probably eighteen. What did you even know at eighteen? I'd been a virgin until Maddy.

So honestly? Nothing. I hadn't known a damn thing.

The second time, you missed that opportunity to love, and well, that was when things went to shit.

Exhibit A: The house. Takeout boxes littered every inch of space, beer bottles totem-poled the boxes, and something smelled.

I sniffed my armpit.

That something was me.

I glanced down the hallway. *Too much effort in trying to get clean. What the hell is the point anyway?* She was gone. Again. I was alone. Again.

And the really sick part?

Before she'd come stomping back into my life, I'd been completely okay with it! I'd finally settled into my job at the local police department. I had great friends, was remodeling my parents' house, and I had the promise of a goat—

Don't ask.

The point? Everything had been fine until Maddy Summers decided to screw me over, again!

The knocking got louder.

"Not home!" I yelled.

The door burst open.

Not my best friend, Max, walked into the house, his feet kicking empty boxes. My best friend, Colton, followed along with Reid, Max's brother, a goat tucked under his arm and his nose scrunched up as if I was the animal, not the crazy mammal he was carrying.

"Dude…" Max shook his head, "…you stink."

Colton winced as a piece of pizza, that had somehow found its way to my ceiling, fell to the ground, narrowly missing his shoes. "Jason…"

"Guys!" I forced a smile. "I'm fine!"

"You're not fine!" Max yelled. "You're a pig in your own filth! You smell, your house is a mess, and I saw at least two good-sized rats leaving through the front door — meaning you've even managed to scare rodents! Pull yourself together!"

I burped. "You gonna slap me now?"

"Do it." Colt crossed his arms. "Or at least hose him off."

"Please!" I shouted. "This from three happily married guys? Let me rot in my filth!"

"He's drunk," Max announced. "He didn't even chase her!"

"What's the point?" I felt the familiar sting of rejection hit me square in the chest. "Things are better this way." I didn't tell them that her car was gone; that when I'd called her work the day after being arrested by my partner at the precinct, she'd taken a week off. And when I'd stopped by her parents', they'd just given me a pathetic look as if they hadn't known what to say.

I should have gotten her number.

I should have run like hell.

"So, go after her." This from Colton.

"And say what? Choose me? Stay with me? She's left me twice, guys. She's not coming back."

I rubbed my chest.

Max sighed and kicked a box in my direction, then reached out and patted my hand. Aw, he was comforting me. That was nice of him to—

"What the hell!" I screamed, as Max slapped me across the face twice then pulled his fist back as if he was going to beat the shit out of me.

"Get off your ass, or so help me God, I'm calling your grandmother!"

"No!" I shot to my feet. "You wouldn't."

Colton shivered. "He would."

"Jason?" an elderly voice chimed in from the door. "Grandma's moving in!"

My eyes widened.

"Those are your choices," Max said, looking pleased. "Either you chase your woman, or Grandma moves in. We already packed her shit."

"What?" Grandma yelled." What was that, Maxy?"

"You look so fit!" He beamed.

She did a little twirl then put on her bright red lipstick. "I've been dancing."

"Oh, it shows." Max winked.

I groaned.

"So, shall we help you shower, or are you and Grandma new roomies?" Colton asked.

I glared at both of them. "Shower. Now."

"That's the spirit!" Max clapped. "Let's go get your woman!"

chapter thirty-three

"The universe never times things well. It's best to always be prepared, which is why I carry around a go-bag with all my essentials. Like, for example, a parka. Because life's a bitch and being caught in a storm naked? Well, you might just get struck by lightning. Nobody wants that. It kills sexual performance. Just ask my friend, Jason Caro. That's spelled J A S O N space C A R O. You'll find his number in the index at the back of the book."

~From Max Emory's Guide to Dating and Other Important Life Lessons

Maddy

My sister officially had the worst timing in the world. She'd shown up, high and drunk off her ass, at my old apartment, screaming my name. Bless my roommates for not calling the cops. They'd let her in and had tried to sober her up. Then they called and told me all about the track marks on her arms.

I took off work, told my parents, and drove into the city, hoping to talk some sense into her one last time. My gut churned at the thought of something happening to Sara. Why did it always feel like the last time whenever I saw her?

It had taken a while to find street parking, so it was getting late. I took the elevator, anxiety filling my veins, making my blood feel cold inside my body. I knocked on the door.

Venus, a gorgeous Asian model who looked too pretty to exist in real life, who also had a heart of gold, answered. Her bow-shaped lips pressed into a thin line as she put her hands on the hips of her low-slung jeans and black belly shirt. The sound of her bangles moving set me on edge even more.

"She's in your old room," she said in a quiet voice. "We tried to get her to sleep it off, but she's a wreck. I don't even want to know what that girl has in her body. She needs a shower, and we left some clean clothes in there for her." Her eyebrows drew together in concern. "Maddy, she's not your problem."

"She's family," I admitted softly. "She'll always be my problem."

I measured the steps to my old bedroom.

Twelve.

I knocked on the door lightly then opened it when I didn't hear an answer.

She was lying face-down on the bare mattress.

I kicked the mattress, as angry tears ran down my cheeks. When she didn't stir, I kicked it again and again.

Finally, she moved to a sitting position and groggily looked up. "Sis?"

"We're going home."

She snorted. "I'm not going anywhere, just partied too hard. I've got a few jobs lined up and—"

"Bullshit!" I screamed, so angry at her, angry at myself, angry at the world, angry that I wasn't home with Jason. Angry that I hadn't given him my number so he wouldn't think I was cutting and running again. "You'll get a job, get your first paycheck, and either inject or snort it — whatever you can find first. You have two choices."

Sara looked away, her eyes distant.

"We either drive home right now, or I drive you to the police station on charges of possession."

She scoffed. "I don't have any drugs on me."

"Doesn't matter. They'll give you a drug test, look at your criminal record, and throw you into jail for a few days while you sober up enough to want to scratch the paint from the walls." I shrugged. "If you go home, we can take you to the rehab center there. It's not as intense as some of the ones in the city."

"I'll think about it." She sniffed and rubbed her nose.

Her blond hair was stringy, her face like a skeleton. I used to want to be her, as a young girl had always looked up to her. All it had taken was one good-looking actor to look her way and offer her party drugs, and she was hooked.

Took them through college to stay alert.

Then took them to find peace and rest.

She fell before she'd even known she'd taken a step.

"You have three seconds." I crossed my arms. "One, two—"

"Why are you such a bitch?" she yelled.

"Because I have to be," I whispered. "Because I need you. Because Annabelle needs you."

Her face lit up.

I knew she still loved her daughter when she wasn't high or drunk. Annabelle was the only good thing she'd accomplished.

"Fine." She stood on shaky stick legs. "I'll go."

We drove back to New Haven in silence.

The shakes started on the outside of town, and then her teeth were chattering uncontrollably, regardless of the coats from the back seat I'd dumped on her. By the time we got to the house, I only had enough time to knock on the door and tell my parents I was taking her for treatment. I had no idea how bad things had gotten and I was worried that keeping her at the house would end up in a 911 call. I asked them to call ahead because her situation kept getting worse.

Withdrawal could kill a person. And she didn't have much on her body anymore.

I felt her head as she leaned against the window, tears streaming down her face as she clenched her teeth.

"I'm sorry."

"It's okay. It's going to be okay."

I wasn't sure I believed it, but I had to be strong for both of us. I hit the accelerator and ran through a red light just as a siren sounded behind me.

Really? I never get a ticket, and now I'm getting pulled over?

"Hold tight." I tucked her in as best I could and hit the down button on my window as a light landed on my face, blinding me.

"Make a habit of running through red lights?" came Jason's smooth voice.

And something about his tone, or maybe the way he smelled, and I just burst into big, fat, ugly tears.

"Whoa, whoa, whoa... It's just a red—" He flashed the light across the seat and pointed it back at me. "What's going on?"

"She was back in the city — said she'd go to rehab — withdrawals—" I hiccupped then tried to calm down, even though I was hyperventilating. When he opened up the car door and pulled me roughly against his chest, I clung to him like he was my lifeline. And he let me.

"I'll escort you. Can you still drive?"

I nodded against his chest.

"You taking her to the center?"

Another nod.

"I'll drive ahead of you. We can get her there in two minutes. They know she's coming?"

I sniffled. "I think my parents called."

"I'll call, too, on my way. Let's go."

And for some stupid reason, I blurted, "Ride like the wind, bulls-eye."

He just stared at me, sadness etched across his features as he nodded. "Ride like the wind."

I'd always told him that before each game; it had been a

joke. We'd loved movies and *Toy Story* had been a personal favorite for no other reason than we'd been best friends since we could talk, and it had been our thing back in the day.

He pressed a hard kiss to my forehead then ran back to his car. Sirens on, he peeled out in front of me.

I hit the accelerator and followed both my heart — and my savior.

chapter thirty-four

"The universe has a funny way of working out the kinks. You give it all your shit, and it goes, 'Look, three gold flecks, I can do something with this.' Nothing is ever forever, and even when you have bad, there's always some good mixed in."

~From Max Emory's Guide to Dating and Other Important Life Lessons

Jason

It had been one of the longest nights of my life. I could see the exhaustion on Maddy's face. I walked her to her door, off-shift, but still in uniform. Her dad answered before she could even touch it.

He took one look at me and asked, "What happened?"

"He saved us," was what Maddy said, when I'd expected her to say something else like, *"Oh, Jason was just doing his job."*

I couldn't speak.

"It's what he does best," her dad answered, and then gave me a nod.

Maddy started to walk in, but I grabbed her arm and pulled her back against my chest.

She slumped against me.

"Stay with me," I whispered in her ear.

She nodded.

The door closed.

And I was carrying her across the chalk line back to my house. Minutes later, I was starting the shower for her.

She was dead on her feet, so I peeled off my uniform, tried to detach my thoughts of her body from my mind, and stepped in the warm water with her.

I washed her breasts.

I washed her stomach.

I kissed her neck.

I couldn't help myself.

"It would have been like this," Maddy whispered against my skin, her lips cold, even with the heat from the water. "It would have been like this, had I not walked away. Nights in the shower together, a partnership… a team."

I hesitated then tilted her chin toward me. "It can still be like this."

"Every day?" Her eyes blurred with tears.

"Every day."

"And the past—"

"Stays where it belongs."

She was kissing me before I could register what was happening. The soap fell from my hands as her tongue slid past my lips, as her hands clenched my back, her nails raking over my hot skin.

Home never felt so right.

So good.

She was igniting a craving in me, as if I'd been in a deep sleep for ten years, and now, suddenly, she was waking me with every brush of her lips. I tilted her body under the hot water, my lips on her neck, licking her skin.

She sighed, "You feel bigger."

I smiled against her neck. "Ten years."

"I know, but…" Her lips parted for me as I stole the next few words from her tongue, the urgency of her touch, even the pressure, my undoing. Maybe even the citrusy taste of her mouth had something to do with it.

Whatever it was, I was a goner.

I was hers.

My body tightened as she ran a feather-light touch of her hands down my chest. I pulled away so I could see her, make sure she was real and not some meltdown I was having, an early mid-life crisis, a dream where I conjured up the one woman who'd gotten away and brought her back to share hot shower sex with her.

"Why are we always wet when we do this?" Her lips were swollen, her voice husky.

With a laugh, I wrapped an arm around her waist and tugged her into me, speaking against her lips. "To be fair, you should always be wet, Maddy…"

Her breath hitched, and that gorgeous red stain lit up her cheeks. I'd missed that, maybe even more than I'd missed my own damn heart all these years.

"I love you." It had sounded more romantic in my head, those three words, but I couldn't wait any longer to get them out. "I never stopped."

Her eyes filled with unshed tears. "Then show me."

"Was the shower and the pool sex not enough? You need more?" I teased, biting down on her bottom lip.

Steam billowed around us as she wrapped her arms around my neck.

I braced us against the wall, my overheated body suddenly frantic to get inside her, to seal what this was between us. To chase it until my eyes burned, and my body demanded sleep. The air was thick with heat and the smell of Irish Spring soap.

"More." She grinned against my mouth.

I kissed her harder, deeper.

"More."

I pressed her body against the tile, our slippery skin sliding across one another. Her nipples were driving me insane with each brush across my naked chest. Once, twice. The water drenched us and started to get cold.

"More."

I couldn't wait any longer.

Because if we stayed longer, we'd freeze.

"Fast," I grit my teeth. "This time, I can't go slow. I can't. Maddy—" Her name fell from my lips, both as a curse and a yearning.

"And next time?"

"So slow you're going to beg for it to be faster…"

Her slick heat was velvet against my tip; one smooth thrust, and I was clawing the tile in an effort to get closer, to fuse our bodies so close together that I'd forget I functioned without her.

"Jason!" Her fingers pressed against my collarbone, and then she wrapped her hands around my shoulders, her mouth slightly open, as her drugged gaze locked on mine. "It never felt like this."

I laughed, pressing her ass firmly against the tile. "I sure hope not. I was only eighteen—"

Her laugh had my body buzzing and zapping with energy, joy, lust. Everything wrapped around us like a warm embrace, as I grinned wickedly at her and pumped harder.

My gaze went from her mouth to the drop of water falling from her chin. My eyes took in her wet hair, swollen mouth, and short gasps for breath. It was the most beautiful thing I'd ever seen.

She was the most beautiful woman I'd ever seen.

And I realized, I'd never really seen anyone but her.

I cupped her face with my hands and kissed her then. I kissed away the anger, the unforgiveness, the betrayal I'd felt. I let it go, laying it across her lips like a promise that I would chase her forever, if that was what it took.

Because she was mine.

She was worth it.

And I wasn't ever going to give up on us, even if I had to go to the depths of Hell and fight every demon in order to free her.

She cried out against my mouth, and I captured each sound with the flick of my tongue, with the pressure of my lips as I tried to make it last, the seconds where everything felt right in the universe. That was the thing about moments of bliss. They end sometimes before they even have time to begin.

I pulled her from the tile then followed, my body shaking under the cold water as she kept pressing small kisses to my lips, my cheeks.

"So…" Maddy laughed a bit, and then her teeth started chattering.

"Yeah?" I couldn't stop staring at her. It was harder than hell to turn away, flick off the shower, and grab a towel. I wished we could have stayed there, pressed against the wall.

I slowly wrapped a white terrycloth towel around her body, then grabbed my own. She tucked herself under my arm as we walked out of the bathroom and into the adjoining master suite.

I should have been surprised to see Max standing there, soap in his hair, looking pissed off, but I wasn't. This was the guy who'd tried to run for mayor of New Haven, just because he'd wanted a reason to make a sign.

So, standing in my bedroom?

Towel wrapped around his waist?

Soap in his hair and, from the twitch in his right eye, maybe there, too?

It should have been expected.

"'Sup, man?" I grinned.

"'Sup. Man." He pointed at his eye. "You took all the hot water! Do you really think that all of this…" he pointed at his body, "…takes only a few minutes under that heat? I need to cook, Jason! My body demands it! What do you expect me to do?"

"Go to a hotel," Maddy offered.

"Grab a hose." My suggestion was less kind.

Max growled, "One does not put cold water on this type of product." He glared at Jason. "Don't you know anything?"

"Sorry, I wasn't paying attention. I was too busy with this one, using all the hot water, longer than seven minutes, I'd say."

Max's face changed, his one eye narrowing. "Nine minutes, at least. Better than last time. I'll give it to you." He grinned, "I take it the graph—"

"Never mind about the graph!" I coughed and pointed to the door. "Now leave."

He turned and then called over his shoulder, "Get some." And then finished with a spanking move before I slammed the door and turned to Maddy.

"He takes some getting used to, kind of like when people used to poison themselves to develop an immunity? Max, here, is like arsenic — small, small, small doses, and you won't die."

Maddy's face spread out into a bright grin. "As long as I get you in big doses, I think I'll be okay."

"Oh yeah?" I walked over to her. I wish I could say I sauntered and looked sexy as hell; instead, I probably looked too eager to get in her arms again. The sloppy grin on my face wasn't helping.

"Yeah." Her eyes darted to mine. "We're doing this."

"Yeah, we are."

I sealed it with a kiss and pulled the towel from her body. I dropped mine to join it in a heap in the middle of the floor.

epilogue

"I'd like to think the universe stops working against us when we start working with it; when we listen to those tiny little hints that maybe our shit stinks a hell of a lot more than we'd originally thought. Spoiler alert — It's not always roses, but it can be if you get your head out of your ass long enough to see the sunshine. Amen."

~From Max Emory's Guide to Dating and Other Important Life Lessons, now a #1 New York Times Bestseller!

Maddy

"CHAMPAGNE!" MAX SHOUTED, slicing off the top of the bottle, his one and only party trick, and shooting it around the yard like it was New Year's instead of our wedding day.

Mine and Jason's. I still couldn't believe it was real. Surrounded by family and friends, I inhaled deeply as my sister winked at me across the pool while she helped Annabelle dangle her feet in.

Sara still struggled. Who wouldn't? But things were slowly getting better, especially after she had gotten a job at one of the local coffee shops. She had more of a purpose and had gained some weight back. More importantly, she had Annabelle.

"You all right?" Jason wrapped his arms around me from behind.

I grabbed his biceps and sighed. "Yeah."

"Party like it's 1999!" Max shouted again, amidst Frank Sinatra music.

"I drugged his coffee," Jason whispered in my ear, causing goose bumps. "He should tucker out in the next hour."

I scoffed, "Wow, Mr. Police Officer, breaking laws left and right?"

"Please, I hire out my crimes." He nodded to Reid who gave him a salute and clinked his bottle with Colt's.

I laughed. "Ah, so they go to jail, and you stay clean.

Smart."

"I thought so."

I pulled his arms away and turned so we were chest to chest. "Thank you."

"For?" His eyes narrowed, his smile staying.

I loved his smile so much. I never wanted to be the cause for it to go away — never again. Rationally, I knew we'd have fights; I knew we'd have things to overcome. I just loved the way it made me feel when he smiled, and especially when that smile was because of us.

"For being you," I teased, just as Max walked over.

Reid, Colt, and the wives followed, a look of trepidation on their faces as if Max was about to face-plant on the knife he was swinging with his hand.

"Jason..." Max held out the knife and a new bottle of champagne, "...will you do the honors?"

Reid paled.

Colt and Milo took a step back as Jason took the knife.

"Should he have sharp objects?" Reid asked, voice weak.

"Do it now," Max encouraged. "Do. It."

Jason rolled his eyes and sliced down the bottle. The top popped off and went flying through the air right into a kid's cheek, literally, right before he was about to kiss some girl behind the tree.

"My face! My face!" he yelled, holding a hand to his cheek.

"I knew it," Max whispered then slapped Jason on the back. "The universe approves of this union, and you're no longer cursed." He wiped a fake tear. "My work here is done." He pounded his chest as he got choked up. "It's done." He lifted his arms and did a slow circle.

The wind picked up.

Jason pulled me closer.

And then Becca was tugging Max by the ear and into her arms.

I didn't ask why she had a goat on a leash, or why a gecko seemed to be riding it.

I'd learned not to ask questions where Max was concerned.

Because for some reason, the guy just existed in a perpetual state of chaos that oddly made sense and, scarily enough, influenced way too many people, if his book sales were to be put into the equation.

"It was nice of you to pick him as your best man." I wrapped an arm around Jason.

"I know." Jason shrugged. "I actually already chose Colt. Then Max threatened to poison him, so Colt stepped down. I don't even want to know where the bachelor party will be."

We'd wanted to get married so fast, he hadn't had time to plan one, so he was going after our honeymoon. The girls and I had every intention of crashing it.

Max disappeared for a few minutes.

And all was forgotten as Jason and I talked to guests.

It was starting to get dark when a giant cake was wheeled out.

Candles were lit and then snuffed out when the top came off the cake, revealing Max, flashing plane tickets around and yelling, "VEGAS!"

"Oh hell," Jason swore. "Max and Vegas… I said never again."

"NEVER, ever," Reid stomped over to us, "Again. He knows what happened last time!"

Colt just shook his head. "Guys, don't worry. I have a plan. We still have all that Xanax…"

I listened in horror as they graphically came up with a

plan that basically involved Max being drugged and lost. Maybe it was because I was in a good mood, or maybe it was because I felt bad for the guy, but I piped up and said, "The girls will go, too. I'll babysit Max."

"If you survive it," Reid said soberly.

"Rest in peace," Colt crossed himself.

Jason pleaded, "Give us a chance, Maddy! Don't throw your life away!"

"I heard you, all of you! You're dead to me." Max's eyes landed on Maddy. "I think I just found my new best friend."

"And just like that, it looks like Colt's back in the game," Jason laughed.

"TRICKERY!" Max roared and then bowed. "Thy name is Jason. You have my respect — but you're still going to Vegas."

"Thought so," Jason grumbled, just as Milo reached her hand into the cake, grabbed a piece, then called his name and threw.

What followed was absolute chaos where Max convinced everyone he was suffocating from chocolate inhalation, and something about Reid having a reaction to Gummy Bears, which earned Max more cake down the throat and up the nose.

While Jason and I sipped champagne under the tree — the one that held our tree house — and watched. Me in my white dress. Him in his tux. And a light summer breeze kissing our skin, swirling around us, like a blessing.

I hope you enjoyed The Consequence of Rejection.

Start at the beginning with Colt and Milo's story, The Consequence of Loving Colton: http://bit.ly/RVDColton

And if you really liked the book I would love a review! If you hated it, same still goes ☺ Stars are stars, and thank you for finishing!

HUGS, RVD

co-ed

About the Book

A college dorm suite…
Four guys and one girl…
No, it's NOT what you are thinking but things do get steamy in here!
Welcome to the NEW Wingmen, Inc.

Releasing April 24!
Pre-Order here: http://bit.ly/RVDCoEd

Excerpt

IT STARTED WITH a really loud moan, the kind that makes your body tingle and your senses so alert you could swear you can actually hear the silence crackling around your face. My heart pounded as I heard another.

I'd been in that stupid dorm for two nights of pure Hell where I watched gross guy after gross guy put socks on their doors and girls do the walk of shame.

It's not my fault I was named Shawn and put in the guys' dorm.

Nor was it my fault that transferring at the beginning of Spring semester meant that they literally had no other rooms for me.

It was this dorm.

Or homelessness.

Okay not really, I could technically find a place, but that would mean rent I couldn't afford unless I found some other sad unfortunate soul willing to live with me and the thing about transferring to the University of Washington at the last minute my Junior year for Softball? Well that meant I literally had no choice but to listen to the moaning.

Only this moan was different.

Really. Different.

The other moans were drunken.

This one sounded… nice.

Not that I ranked moans on a scale from one to ten.

But if I did, it would be a solid seven, maybe an eight.

The moan was longer this time.

I shot up from my bed and listened.

"Go back to sleep." The gruff voice came from the other side of the room where my very male and very metrosexual roommate slept with a stuffed unicorn and a humidifier that made weird puffing noises because of his apparent dust allergies.

"Do you hear that?" I whispered.

He flipped over on his side giving me a generous view of his six pack and plaid pajama pants. I'd think he was attractive if he wasn't so bossy, the first day I unpacked my bags I could feel his judgement over every thing I placed in my drawer like it wasn't folded well enough to deserve a spot.

"Everyone on the floor heard that. Seriously, sleep, you came here with dark circles under your eyes and they're just going to get worse if you lay in your bed listening to the threesome across the way do their jobs."

My ears perked. "Threesome? Jobs?"

He put the white unicorn over his face and screamed into it. What? Like I was the one being disruptive? I had practice at five am! It was one in the morning, some of us needed uninterrupted sleep!

"Shawn," He said my name with a bit of disdain, to be fair he thought his new roommate was going to be less annoying than the last and at least packing a penis. I'd like to think he was right about the first, and very irritated about the penis.

What? Like it's my fault I was born a girl? "Just, try to go back to sleep, it's Friday, which means it's going to be a long night of moaning, if you need ear plugs I have a spare in my desk."

"For situations like this?" Seriously? "They give them out for free. Everyone knows it's necessary."

"Why the hell is it necessary?" My interest was more than peaked.

"Oh. My. Hell. What did I do? What? So I dumped her because she had a big middle toe! Everyone has their deal breakers! Big deal!" Slater threw his pillow on to the ground and then stood raking his hands through his hair, pacing, like a mad man. Apparently he had a thing about sleep, and apparently I just made him irrationally angry over a break up. "I mean so what? Is this God's way of punishing me?" He looked up to the ceiling. "You give me a girl who can't even sleep through a few moans and doesn't even wash her face before bed, Kill me now!"

I gulped. "Hey, you okay?"

"No," he glared over at me. "I'm not okay," I think the mocking air quotes gave it away. "I'm exhausted and I need my sleep and you talk more than my Aunt Gertrude who literally won't even stop talking during mass."

"Sorry?"

He inhaled deeply through his nostrils. "Look, I know you're curious, all the newbies are. I'm going to give you the short version, all right?"

"Um, okay." I sat up straighter. he crooked his finger and walked over to the door that led to the living space separating us from their room.

I'd never seen a place so big and nice at a University, again another reason why I was still putting up with the moans. I had a legit living space and a shared kitchen and my own bathroom.

Plus, it's not like Slater was a slob.

He actually alphabetized his stuff.

And labeled hair products.

I slowly got up from the bed and walked over to where he stood by the door.

He looked up at me. "You're tall for a woman."

"You're short for a man." I fired back.

He just grinned. "Eh maybe you aren't so bad, and I'm not short, I'm five ten, you're the monster here."

"Six foot, big deal." I shrugged, guys always had a problem with my height but Slater seemed to be impressed by it, not intimidated, "So what's the story?"

He opened the door a crack just as another moan rang out. He bit down on his lip as three moans followed and then a slight scream. "In three, two, one."

The door across from us opened.

A beautiful girl stretched her arms over her head and then cracked her neck, she was wearing jeans and a white crop top and had her dark curly hair pulled up into a big ponytail. "Thanks guys, you always know how to work me."

I sucked in a breath just as Slater slapped a hand over my mouth. "Don't give us away, they dont like spies."

"They? What? Like the cold war's taking place in the space between us?" I rolled my eyes.

He didn't. "Watch."

A tall guy with lazy green eyes and a man bun stepped out and crossed his arms, he had his skinny jeans riding so low on his hips it was almost indecent, and of course he had no shirt on.

So what? They were having sex?

Another guy stepped out, blond hair, killer abs, same outfit, like it was a uniform or something, and then another one followed, he was the one that made my heart do a weird thud. He was tall, like really tall. At least six foot six, with more muscles than I knew existed on another human and a deadly smile that looked slightly crooked, and of course one small dimple on the right side of his mouth, and blond locks that hung past his ears. Were they all descendants of Thor or something? Trying out for Vikings? Game of Thrones? Where does an individual find that many good looking men? And what monster puts them in the same room together?

The guy looked like Charlie Hunnam and Brad Pitt got it on. I almost couldn't look away.

"They have that effect on all their clients." Slater whispered. He was still there? I hadn't noticed. "And before you start lusting, remember, they don't date, they don't kiss, they… please."

"Come again?" I whispered.

"Oh they do, and often." His stupid response. "I mean they have this weird no intercourse rule but last year rumor had it that three girls orgasmed by one of the guys holding a box of cheerios."

"Shut up." I hissed.

Slater held up his hands. "Don't shoot the messenger."

"So, they… please girls." I licked my lips, disgusting, who made a job out of that? And three of them? Wasn't that awkward.

One of them, the blond sexy one leaned down and kissed the side of the girl's neck while the other two flanked each side, they all touched her intimately, but not in a way that was overtly sexual, almost like they just wanted to show her they were close, oh and you know, share an insane amount of body heat.

She closed her eyes and fell back while the tall one tilted her chin up and whispered. "Make sure you hydrate and text us if you need anything else."

She slipped something into his hands and honest to God, stumbled towards the door like their love was her drug or something.

It clicked shut.

Slater put his forefinger on my chin and shut my gaping mouth just as all three of them looked across the room and smiled.

I should have dodged that smile. Should have slammed the door in disgust. Instead I was so damn intrigued I opened it wider, and glared.

"No, no! They like a challenge, don't just—" Slater was already pulling me back. I crossed my arms and stared them down. And then I realized I was in nothing but a sports bra and a see through tank top.

They looked their fill.

I felt hot all over.

Finally Slater was able to pull me back into the room, slamming the door shut behind him and locking it for good measure. "Stay. Away."

I gave my head a shake. "Trust me I'm not into sharing and I don't date during the season."

He scoffed. "They don't date either, they have loads of rules. I've seen them convert a girl destined for the convent, so you can see why I'm concerned that your pulse just picked up."

"It did not!" I gulped.

He pressed his hand to my neck and swore. "Don't lie to your new roommate, it's rude."

I slapped his hand away. "I thought you hated me because I have boobs."

"Oh I love boobs." He grinned widely. "I just dont want

yours, I'm not into taller girls or ones who happen to be my roommate when I specifically asked for a quiet athlete whose cleanliness was better than Steve." He shrugged.

"Steve?"

"All Steves are dirty, they should just know these things, and Steve used to clip his toenails onto the floor just sprinkled them around like fairy dust, and don't even get me started on CrossFit Steve's calluses and his joy in ripping them off and showing me just how big one chunk of skin could be. Oh right and he typically did this before dinner, how else do you think I got the abs?"

I snorted out a laugh. "So CrossFit Steve's both your curse and your inspiration?"

I could have sworn his eye twitched before he gave his head a shake. "I can tell you're one of the good ones, don't fall for it. Stay far, far, far away, in fact, you should move." He eyed me up and down. "How do you feel about Siberia."

I walked back to my bed. "I'm not moving to Siberia because I'm living in the same dorm with some weird Co-Eds who like to please women."

"Women, men, plants, my Grandma, they'll do it all for a price, and often, together. Just… stay away."

He moved back to his bed and pulled his duvet over his face. I heard a muffled sigh and then he threw them back over his body and stared me down. "I mean it, the pleasure ponies are bad news."

I burst out laughing. "Please tell me thats their real name!"

He joined in. "Nah, thats my nice nickname for them… The real company name is under Wingmen Inc."

I stilled. "The Matchmaking company that Facebook tried to buy out last year?"

He nodded. “Both gurus wanted to leave a legacy, hand-picked those three to work for them here at the university, when one graduates, another’s nominated, let’s just put it this way, those guys? Raking it in… no shame whatsoever.”

“But how? Why?”

He yawned. “Because we live in a world full of broken hearts and everyone wants to be told the lie.”

I felt small, like I wanted to crawl into my bed and cry a bit. “What lie?”

“That it’s not you, it’s them, that the world will give you better, that you’ll get your happily ever after, that life is like the movies — that we dont live in a sea full of broken fucked hearts.”

We stopped talking after that.

I laid awake for two more hours wondering if he could see my insecurity, my pain. And wondering how I was going to hide it from the ones who promised to fix it—for a price.

Releasing April 24!
Pre-Order here: http://bit.ly/RVDCoEd

the consequence series

the consequence of loving colton

It's all fun and games…until someone's heart is broken.

They're not kids anymore, but Milo Caro is certain that Colton Mathews will only see her as his best friend's little sister for the rest of their lives. After all, he made that clear the night before she left for college. But four years later, her brother is getting married and Colt's the best man—and guess who is the best man's last-minute date?

Milo vows to use the wedding to either claim the smoldering firefighter's heart or douse this torch for good. When Max—her best friend from college, who may be carrying a torch of his own—crashes the party, they devise a plan to make Colt see what he's missing. But after Colt catches on, he decides to cook up his own revenge.

Now it's personal. Colt and Milo are at war, and between Max's questionable acting methods, an unfortunate trip to jail, and a maniacal fiancée, what could possibly go right?

the consequence of rejection

He may have devastatingly good looks, an abundance of charm, and a claim to one of the biggest hotel empires around, but he has no ambition anymore. So when his fed-up friends decide they've had enough of his moping, they sign him up to be the next bachelor on the reality series *Love Island*. And between his pride and his forged signature on an ironclad contract, Max just can't say no.

Now he's stranded in paradise with twenty-four women, one terrifying goat, and Becca, the breathtaking barista who already turned him down back home. The closer Max gets to Becca, the more determined he becomes to win her over. As she gets to know him better, things start heating up. But is Becca really after Max's heart—or is she after the cash prize she could claim once the cameras stop rolling?

the consequence of seduction

Reid Emory has never had reason to question his luck with the ladies. As the owner of a lethal set of aqua-blue eyes and a devastating grin, this Hollywood heartthrob always brings his A game…but lately his luck seems to have run out. The actor is in need of some help, and there's only one person he can trust to take his love life—and his career—to an explosive new level.

Jordan Litwright's newest client is trying her patience. As a publicist, she's more than content to stay in the background and let others shine. But when a publicity stunt backfires, she suddenly finds herself thrust into the spotlight—as Reid's new love interest. And while other men usually overlook her, Reid is focusing in with laserlike intensity. There's no denying they have serious chemistry.

But once Reid breaks into the big time, can they turn their made-for-the-media romance into a forever love?

acknowledgements

I FEEL SO blessed every time I release a new book, and this is no different. God is so good and I am so thankful that I'm able to do what I love every day! Thank you to all the readers and bloggers who make this possible. I can't thank you enough and I will forever be in your debt! I'm going to keep this one short because honest moment, I'm sitting in LA looking out at Hollywood BLVD after a movie premiere of one of my books and my brain is still a bit on fire. I'm sitting here FULLY aware that the only reason I'm able to do this is because you guys, the readers, are buying books and are enjoying them, so from the bottom of my heart, thank you. Thank you for caring. Thank you for sharing. Thank you for being you and loving books just as much as I do! I'm forever in your debt.

Hugs, RVD

about the author

Rachel Van Dyken is a *New York Times*, *Wall Street Journal*, and *USA Today* bestselling author. When she's not writing about hot hunks for her Regency romance or New Adult fiction books, Rachel is dreaming up *new* hunks. (The more hunks, the merrier!) While Rachel writes a lot, she also makes sure she enjoys the finer things in life—like *The Bachelor* and strong coffee.

Rachel lives in Idaho with her husband, son, and two boxers. Fans can follow her writing journey at www.RachelVanDykenAuthor.com and www.facebook.com/rachelvandyken.

also by rachel van dyken

Eagle Elite
Elite
Elect
Entice
Elicit
Bang Bang
Enchant
Enforce
Ember
Elude
Empire
Enrage
Eulogy

The Bet Series
The Bet
The Wager
The Dare

Seaside Series
Tear
Pull
Shatter
Forever
Fall
Strung
Eternal

Seaside Pictures
Capture
Keep
Steal

Waltzing With The Wallflower
Waltzing with the Wallflower
Beguiling Bridget
Taming Wilde

London Fairy Tales
Upon a Midnight Dream
Whispered Music
The Wolf's Pursuit
When Ash Falls

Renwick House
The Ugly Duckling Debutante
The Seduction of Sebastian St. James
The Redemption of Lord Rawlings
An Unlikely Alliance
The Devil Duke Takes a Bride

Ruin Series
Ruin
Toxic
Fearless
Shame

The Consequence Series
The Consequence of Loving Colton
The Consequence of Revenge
The Consequence of Seduction
The Consequence of Rejection

The Dark Ones Series
The Dark Ones
Untouchable Darkness
Dark Surrender
Darkest Temptation

Wingmen Inc.
The Matchmaker's Playbook
The Matchmaker's Replacement

The Bachelors of Arizona
The Bachelor Auction
The Playboy Bachelor
The Bachelor Contract

Curious Liaisons
Cheater
Cheater's Regret

Players Game
Fraternize
Infraction

Other Titles
The Parting Gift
Compromising Kessen
Savage Winter
Divine Uprising
Every Girl Does It
RIP

RACHEL VAN DYKEN BOOKS

www.rachelvandykenauthor.com

Made in the USA
San Bernardino,
CA

57581331R00146